THE
WEIGHT
OF OUR
SKY

THE WEIGHT OF OUR SKY

HANNA ALKAF

SALAAM
READS

NEW YORK   LONDON   TORONTO   SYDNEY   NEW DELHI

An imprint of Simon & Schuster Children's Publishing Division
1230 Avenue of the Americas, New York, New York 10020

For information about special discounts for bulk purchases, please contact Simon & Schuster Special Sales at 1-866-506-1949 or business@simonandschuster.com.
The Simon & Schuster Speakers Bureau can bring authors to your live event. For more information or to book an event, contact the Simon & Schuster Speakers Bureau at 1-866-248-3049 or visit our website at www.simonspeakers.com.
Jacket design by Krista Vossen
Interior design by Hilary Zarycky
The text for this book was set in Sabon.
Manufactured in the United States of America
First Edition
2 4 6 8 10 9 7 5 3 1
Library of Congress Cataloging-in-Publication Data
Names: Hanna Alkaf, author.
Title: The weight of our sky / Hanna Alkaf.
Description: First edition. | New York : Salaam Reads, [2019]
Summary: "Amid the Chinese-Malay conflict in Kuala Lumpur in 1969, sixteen-year-old Melati must overcome prejudice, violence, and her own OCD to find her way back to her mother"—Provided by publisher.
Identifiers: LCCN 2018012693 (print) | LCCN 2018018991 (eBook)
ISBN 9781534426085 (hardcover) | ISBN 9781534426108 (eBook)
Subjects: | CYAC: Obsessive-compulsive disorder—Fiction. | Mental illness—Fiction. | Race riots—Fiction. | Malays (Asian people)—Fiction. | Chinese—Malaysia—Fiction. | Ethnic relations—Fiction. | Kuala Lumpur (Malaysia)—History—20th century—Fiction.
Classification: LCC PZ7.1.H36377 (eBook)
| LCC PZ7.1.H36377 Wei 2019 (print) | DDC [Fic]—dc23
LC record available at https://lccn.loc.gov/2018012693

For Malik and Maryam,
as proof that dreams do come true.
For Umar, without whom this one wouldn't have.
And for anak-anak Malaysia everywhere.

AUTHOR'S NOTE

Before I even begin to say anything else, I'm going to say this: This book is not a light and easy read, and in the interest of minimizing harm, I'd like to warn you now that its **contents include graphic violence, death, racism, OCD, and anxiety triggers.** If any of this is distressing for you at this time, I'd recommend either waiting until you're in the right space to take all of that on or forgoing it altogether.

Is that weird, for an author to basically say, "Please don't read my book"? Maybe. But I mean it. **If this will hurt you, please don't read my book.** No book is worth sacrificing your own well-being for.

Are you still here?

Did you get this far?

If you did, thank you. I appreciate you. I would have, whether or not you'd kept going, but I'm even more grateful because it wasn't so long ago that a book like this would never even have made it as far as an editor's desk, much less exist in the tangible, typeset form you hold in your hands right now, a dream made real.

I appreciate you because you will now bear witness to the events that have shaped my beloved Malaysia into the country it is today: The events of May 13, 1969, when, in the wake of a contentious general election when opposition parties won unexpected victories at the expense of the ruling coalition, the Malays and the Chinese clashed in a bloody battle in the streets of Kuala Lumpur, in flames and fury stoked by political interest. One week later, the death toll climbed to 196—the official number, though Western diplomatic sources at the time suggested it was closer to 600—and the powers that be had an excuse to put policies in place that differentiated between racial groups and kept those at the top firmly, comfortably aloft on airy cushions of privilege, policies with repercussions we still live with to this day.

I appreciate you because without your eyes, your attention, your willingness to listen, as the memories and voices of those who lived through it begin to fade, this seminal point in our past becomes nothing more than a couple of paragraphs in our textbooks, lines stripped of meaning, made to regurgitate in exams and not to stick in your throat and pierce your heart with the intensity of its horror.

I appreciate you because this is our story, and without an audience, a story dies. And we cannot afford to let it.

I can't say all of what you're about to read is true; this is a work of fiction, after all, and even in nonfiction, so much relies on the memories of traumatized survivors and the words of those who write the history books, and both of those can lie. So I will say that many, many hours of research went into this, including wading through reams of articles both academic and non-, first-person interviews, expert advice, and more. You'll notice themes you might find unbelievable in a modern context, like the fact that Melati would believe she's being controlled by a djinn instead of consulting a mental health professional. But this was 1969: There was little treatment available for OCD in Kuala Lumpur then, and even if there was, there was also a heavy cloud of stigma associated with seeing a psychiatrist, with many believing they would be institutionalized— or worse still, lobotomized—for "being crazy." It wasn't uncommon then to seek traditional or religious treatment for illnesses you couldn't quite explain to your regular doctor; in fact, it's not uncommon now, either.

As you read, you may also want to keep in mind that for Muslims, djinn are real. They aren't just wacky blue creatures with a Robin Williams voice, or mythical beings that pour out of old lamps and ancient rings to grant you three wishes; they exist for us in ways that they may not for you.

And now that I have said all this, I leave it to you, dear reader, to forge on and make of this story what you will.

I appreciate you. Still. Always.

Love,
Hanna

CHAPTER ONE

BY THE TIME SCHOOL ENDS on Tuesday, my mother has died seventeen times.

On the way to school, she is run over by a runaway lorry, her insides smeared across the black tar road like so much strawberry jelly. During English, while we recite a poem to remember our parts of speech ("An interjection cries out HARK! I need an EXCLAMATION MARK!" our teacher Mrs. Lalitha declaims, gesturing for us to follow, pulling the most dramatic faces), she is caught in a cross fire between police and gang members and is killed by a stray bullet straight through her chest, blood blossoming in delicate blooms all over her crisp white nurse's uniform. At recess, she accidentally ingests some sort of dire poison and dies screaming in agony, her face purple, the corners of her open mouth flecked with white foam and spittle. And as we peruse our geography textbooks, my mother is stabbed repeatedly by robbers, the wicked blades of their parangs gliding through her flesh as though it were butter.

I know the signs; this is the Djinn, unfolding himself, stretching out, pricking me gently with his clawed fingers. *See what I can do?* he whispers, unfurling yet another death scene in all its technicolor glory. *See what happens when you disobey?* They float to the top of my consciousness unbidden at the most random times and set off a chain reaction throughout my entire body: cold sweat, damp palms, racing heart, nausea, light-headedness, the sensation of a thousand needles pricking me from head to toe.

It seems difficult now to believe that there was ever a time when the only djinns I believed in came from fairy tales, benevolent creatures that poured like smoke from humble old oil lamps and antique rings, granted you your heart's desire, then disappeared when the transaction was complete. I might even have daydreamed of finding one someday. And later, they took a different shape, one informed by religious teachers and Quran recitation classes: creatures of smoke and fire, who had their own realm on Earth and kept to themselves, for the most part.

I didn't realize they could be sharp, cruel, insidious little things that crept and wormed their way into your thoughts and made your brain hot and itchy.

The clanging of the final bell echoes through the school corridors. "Te-ri-ma-ka-sih-cik-gu." The class singsongs their thank-yous in unison as Mrs. Lim nods and strides briskly out the door in her severe, high-necked navy-blue dress, the blackboard covered in complicated mathematical formulas, the floor before it covered in chalk dust. I stuff my books hurriedly into my bag, smiling half-heartedly and waving as other girls pass—"Bye, Mel!" "See you tomorrow!"—and I concentrate on the task at hand. *Biggest to smallest, pencil case in the right-hand pocket, tap each item three times before closing the bag, one, two, three.* Something feels off. My hands are frozen, suspended above my belongings. Did I do that right? Did I tap three times or four? I break out into a light sweat. *Again*, the Djinn whispers, *again. Think how much better you'll feel when you finally get it.*

No, I tell him firmly, trying to ignore the way my fingers twitch, the wave of panic rising from my stomach.

Yes, he says.

One, two, three. One, two, three. One, two . . .

"Well?"

I look up, startled. My best friend, Safiyah, is standing by my desk, rocking back and forth eagerly on her heels, quivering with high excitement from the tips of her toes to the tip of her perfectly perky ponytail, tied back with a length of white ribbon. "Perfectly perky" is actually a great description of Saf in general, whom my mother often jokes only ever has two modes: "happy" and "asleep." She bounces away through her days, dispensing ready smiles, compliments, and high fives to all and sundry, while I trail along in her wake, awkward, vaguely melancholy, and in a constant state of semi-embarrassment.

I'm pretty sure Saf is the reason I have friends at all.

"Well, what?"

Saf's face falls. "Don't tell me you forgot! You, me, Paul? Remember?"

"Oh, that." My heart sinks. The last thing I want to do right now is be trapped in the dark, stuffy recesses of the neighborhood cinema as everyone else watches one movie and the Djinn forces me to watch another.

"Do we really have to, Saf?" I sling my bag over my shoulder and make for the door. *One, two, three. One, two, three. One, two, three.* There is a very specific pattern to adhere to, a rhythm that's smooth and soothing, like the waltzes Mama likes to listen to on the radio on Sunday afternoons. A method to the madness.

Not that this is madness. It's the Djinn.

"Of course we do!" Saf scurries along beside me, taking two steps for every one of my strides. "You promised! And anyway, I always back you up when it's something to do with *your* Paul. . . ."

"You leave Paul McCartney out of this." Right foot first out the door—good. "Or any of the Beatles, for that matter," I add as an afterthought. I mean, I'm a little iffy about Ringo, but even *he's* better than Paul Newman.

One, two, three. One, two, three. One, two, three.

"Come on, Mel, please. . . ." Her tone is wheedling now. "You know it has to be today. My dad's at some kind of meeting until late. He'll never let me go otherwise. You know how he feels about movies." She screws up her face and lowers her voice in a dead-on imitation of her father. "'Movies? Movies DULL the mind, Safiyah. They are the refuge of the UNCULTURED and the UNEDUCATED. They erode your MORALS.'"

I snort with laughter in spite of myself. "Fine," I say grudgingly. "It's not like Mama expects me at home anyway; she's on shift at the hospital until tonight. But can't we go to Cathay or Pavilion? At least they aren't so far. We could just walk."

Saf shakes her head firmly. "The Rex," she says. "We have to go to the Rex."

I shoot her a glance. "This wouldn't have anything to do with the fact that Jason's father's sugarcane stall happens to be right across the street from there, right?"

"I don't know what you're talking about," Saf says innocently, playing with the frayed end of her hair ribbon and doing her best not to look at me, a blush spreading like wildfire across her dimpled cheeks. "I just . . . really happen to prefer watching movies at the Rex." I can't help but grin. Saf can fool a lot of people with those good-girl looks and that demure smile. But then again most people haven't been friends with her since the age of seven, when she marched right up to me on the first day of primary school, while everyone else stood around looking nervous and unsure, and declared cheerfully, "I like you! Let's be best friends." On the surface, we're polar opposites: She is bright where I am dim, cheery smiles where I am worried frowns, pleasing plumpness where I am sharp, uncomfortable angles. But maybe that's why we fit together so perfectly.

"You are so obvious," I snigger, jabbing her in the ribs, and we dissolve into giggles as we run for the bus.

I hoist myself up the steps—right foot first: good girl, Mel—and the Djinn suddenly rears up, ready and alert. I feel a sickening weight in my stomach. The right-hand window seat in the third row, my usual choice—the safest choice—is occupied. A Chinese auntie, her loose short-sleeved blouse boasting dark patches of sweat, dozes in the afternoon heat. Whenever she leans too far forward, she quickly jerks her head back, her eyes opening for a split second, her face rearranging itself into something resembling propriety. But before long, she's nodding off again, lulled by the gentle rolling of the bus.

I can feel the panic start to descend, that telltale prickling starting in my toes and working its way up to claim the rest of me. *If you don't sit in that seat, the safe seat, Mama will die*, the Djinn whispers, and I hate how familiar his voice is to my ears, that low, rich rasp like gravel wrapped in velvet. *Mama will die, and it'll be all your fault.*

I know it doesn't make sense. I know it shouldn't matter. But at the same time, I am absolutely certain that nothing matters more than this, not a single thing in the entire world. My chest heaves, up and down, up and down.

Quickly, I slide into the window seat on the left—still third row, which is good, but on the left, which is most definitely, terribly, awfully not good. But I can make it right. I can make it safe.

The old blue bus coughs and wheezes its way down the road and as Saf waxes lyrical about the dreamy swoop of Paul Newman's perfect hair and the heavenly blue of his perfect eyes, my mother is floating, floating, floating down into the depths of the Klang River, her face blue, her eyes shut, her lungs filled with murky water.

Quickly, quietly, so that Saf won't notice, I tap my right foot, then my left, then right again, thirty-three sets of three altogether, all the way to Petaling Street.

Finally, the Djinn subsides. For now.

CHAPTER TWO

"WE'VE GOT SOME TIME," SAF says as the bus deposits us on the corner and rumbles off down the road. "Wanna go listen to some records?"

"Sure," I say, "but I have to make a call first."

Saf rolls her eyes. "Again?"

"You know I have to, Saf," I say, feeling around in my pocket for a ten-cent coin. "You know my mom always wants me to check in after school."

"Fine," she grumbles, and we head for a nearby pay phone. I grab the receiver and push my coin into the slot, hearing the *clink* as it rolls down into the depths of the machine. Saf hangs back a few paces, waiting for me to finish.

Three beeps, and then nothing.

I start to sweat. *Come on, come on*, I think, fishing around in the depths of my bag for another coin. In the distance, Saf pulls monstrous faces at me, and I stick my tongue out at her in return, trying my best to quell the panic rising in my throat, threatening to choke me. Mama falls to her death from a great height, her body hitting the ground with a *thud* that echoes through my head.

I dial the number again.

Come on, come on, come on.

The Djinn howls, and I tap my feet quickly, right first, then shifting left, trying to appease him. *Three, six, nine, twelve, fifteen . . .*

"Hello?"

Relief floods through me. "Hello! Umm, hello. Can I speak to Nurse Salmah, please?"

"Is that you, Melati, darling?" I recognize the raspy, sandpapery voice of Auntie Tipah, Mama's friend and colleague, who goes through half a dozen cigarettes a day— "Never in front of the patients, though, darlings, hand on heart!"—and swears she'll quit each week.

"Yes, ma'am. Just checking in."

"Same time every day. You're better than any alarm clock I've ever had! Hold on, I'll get her."

Another pause; I quickly fill it with numbers. *Three, six, nine . . .*

"Hi, Melati."

"Hi, Mama!" *She's alive. She's alive!* My whole body sags with relief, and for a moment, I allow myself to breathe.

It lasts about ten seconds. Because of course I should

know better by now. The relief never lasts. The threat of death still hovers, like a shadow I can't shake. The Djinn still demands his price.

"Everything okay?" she asks, the way she does every time I call. The sound of her voice and the familiar rhythm of our daily ritual soothes me. She isn't hurt. She isn't dead. Everything is okay.

"Yup." I clutch the receiver, pressing it close to my ear, twirling the cord tightly in my fingers. "Everything's fine. Are you okay?"

"Yes, sayang, I'm fine. A little tired. I'm on shift tonight; I'll be home late. Mak Siti has your dinner, okay?"

"Okay." I make a face, even though I know she can't see me; Mak Siti is our neighbor, and dinner with her means rice, a meager slice of fried fish, and a watery broth filled with wilted vegetables, all eaten to the accompaniment of the meowing of five cats and a litany of complaints, criticisms, and grouses.

"Don't complain." I can hear her smiling; she knows what I'm thinking.

"I'm not! I'm going to the movies with Saf, okay?"

"On a Tuesday?"

"Yeah, her father isn't home." Mama knows all about Pakcik Adnan and his rules.

There's a pause. "Are you sure you'll be okay?"

What is it about mothers? The woman is psychic.

"I'll be okay, I think," I say, twirling the cord tight around my fingers, watching them go from pink to white. "I might call again later, though."

"Fine, but don't go home too late, and make sure you do your homework."

"Okay. Bye, Mama. Love you."

"Bye, sayang."

I hang up feeling much better. The numbers have done their job. Mama is safe.

Or is she?

Did I miss something? Was there a tiny pause before she said, "I'm fine"? Did she sound sick or hurt? I run over the entire conversation again in my head, sifting through the words for hidden meanings and missed clues. It feels as if the Djinn's sharp teeth are gnawing away at my frayed nerves as I hover at the phone booth indecisively, biting my bottom lip. Is she really safe? Should I call her again, just to be sure?

Do it, he whispers. *You'll feel better. What's the harm? Make the call.*

I pick up the receiver again, the plastic still warm from my hand, my fingers poised to dial.

Then I set it down again with a *bang*. From where she stands a few steps away, Saf looks up at me, startled by the sudden noise, and I try to shoot her a smile. *No*, I think to myself firmly. *Mama is fine. You talked to her; you heard her yourself, telling you everything is okay. Don't listen to him and his lies.*

I walk away on leaden feet, trying my hardest not to look back.

The numbers started out as a game, as they so often do for little children. If I can win three games of "one, two, jus" in a row, concentrating hard to anticipate Saf's rock, paper, or scissors, then Abah will let me listen to that scary show on the radio. If I make it home from the bus stop in exactly twenty-seven steps, then Mama will have made my favorite bubur cha cha for tea, sweet and hot and laden with sweet potatoes and yams and bananas. If I can lastik at least five geckos off the wall, fashioning a makeshift slingshot out of my fingers and the orange rubber bands that came wrapped around our rolled-up newspapers each morning, then they'll let me stay up late tonight. When it worked, it was a tiny act of magic, a small miracle that only fueled my belief in the power of the numbers; when it didn't—and, of course, it didn't, more often than not—it only meant that I'd been doing it wrong.

Most people grow out of it, this belief in magic, this reliance on little wonders, and I did too. But then Abah died, and in the echoing space he left behind inside me, the Djinn rushed in, making himself comfortable, latching onto those old familiar cues. He started off slowly:

If you tap your toothbrush against the sink three times before you brush, if you take exactly twelve steps to get from your bed to the kitchen, if you flick the light switch on and off six times before bed, then Mama stays well and happy and healthy. And if you've accepted that, as I did, then it's not that much of a leap to think: *If you DON'T do these things, then Mama will NOT stay well and happy and healthy. Mama will die.* And if you've accepted that, then it begins to consume you. That's all you think about.

It's been six months since I first told Mama about the strange, frightening thoughts that had started seeping into my brain, wrestled it into submission, and taken over every inch, filling it with dark, blood-soaked images of death. *Her* death.

I'd slipped into her room after she'd come home from work, the room she used to share with Abah but was now hers alone. My stomach was a tight cluster of knots, my head filled with numbers. Every step that brought me closer to her door, the voice in my ear screamed: *She'll disown you, she'll push you away, she'll think you're dangerous and have you carted off to the madhouse.*

No, she won't, I remember thinking to myself. Mama could always make everything better, from skinned knees to bruised hearts. Why would this be any different?

You're about to tell your own mother you imagine her dying—how can that be normal? She'll think you're crazy;

she'll toss you into a mental asylum and leave you there to rot.

The voice chipped away my confidence, exposing my weaknesses in a crisscrossing map of scars and wounds. I moved about her room, arranging the ornaments on her dresser, the makeup on her vanity, lining them just so, fidgety and restless and wanting desperately to throw up.

"What is it, sayang?" she asked me gently, putting a hand out to stroke my arm. *Tell her*, I thought to myself. *Tell her; you'll feel better.*

So I blurted it out. All of it: the endless thoughts of her death, the constant counting and tapping and pacing that kept me up at night for fear that doing them wrong meant that I'd wake up in the morning to find her stiff and lifeless in her bed.

And she'd recoiled.

Oh, she pretended she hadn't. She tried to recover quickly, pulling me in for a reassuring hug. But I'd seen her eyes widen in . . . fear? Disgust? I'd seen her flinch and turn away. I'd seen her pull her hand back for a minute, as if worried I'd contaminate her, or hurt her. Or worse.

"Don't worry, Melati," she'd told me, holding me close. "We'll find a way to get through this. We'll get help. I'll make it all better, you'll see."

I let her comfort me and tried to forget the look I'd just seen in her eyes.

• • •

Petaling Street is rarely quiet, and today is no exception. The sea of tattered rainbow umbrellas and striped red-and-white canopies offers minimal relief from the piercing afternoon sun. Beneath them, shoppers, wanderers, dreamers, and hustlers weave in and out among cars, motorcycles, trishaws, and a parade of vendors peddling their wares. "Fresh bananas," an old man yells hoarsely, "Come and try my fresh bananas! Cheap, cheap!" From another corner comes the melancholy cry of the man in black, who calls, "Manja, manja . . ." to all the girls who pass, trying to entice them with the table full of powders and potions before him, each promising more luscious hair, whiter teeth, or a second look from a certain special boy. . . . The air is thick with a pungent mix of odors: the delectable aroma wafting from the famous shredded duck buns on the one side; the mysterious smells that emanate from the jars and boxes that line the shelves of the Chinese medicine hall; the heady, overwhelming cologne that trails behind the college boys swaggering down the sidewalk in their ill-fitting drainpipe trousers, combs stuck in their back pockets; and everywhere, a faint undercurrent of stale sweat and cigarette smoke.

On days like today, when I'm surrounded by people of every shape and size and color, I often stare at passersby and wonder if they're all being tormented by their own djinns. Maybe that mother in the orange sari tugging impatiently on her little girl's hand as they exit the sundry shop is irritable because she can't stop thinking about how dirty and dusty everything is, can't stay the aching need to scrub every inch of both her child's body and her own. Maybe that young man so desperate to speak to the pretty young woman next to him at the bus stop is really doing it because he's trying to save her from an unspeakable fate dictated by the monster inside him. I can't tell just by looking, but maybe they've learned to hide their demons too.

Or maybe they really are happy and contented, with minds that tick along from one thought to another, without taking any meandering detours, or getting lost on highways with no exits, or going round and round in unending loops.

Must be nice.

We've barely walked ten steps before our flimsy school blouses are soaked through with sweat. "I need a drink," Saf moans, rolling her eyes and clutching my arm as she pretends to swoon. "I'm not going to make it, Melati, I'm just not. Don't forget me, okay?" She whirls around, looking me square in the eyes. "Speak my name. Tell my story!" Around us, people are looking over and grinning at her antics, and I can feel my face growing hot with embarrassment.

"Was that really necessary?" I mutter through gritted teeth.

"Absolutely," she says airily, tossing her ponytail and making a beeline for the air mata kucing stall a few feet ahead of us. "Should've seen the look on your face."

While we wait in line, I find myself mesmerized by the fortune-teller across the street. An old Indian man clad in a striped green shirt and loose gray trousers, he sits at a folding card table, a bright green parrot in a bamboo cage by his side. With each customer who sits before him, he taps on the cage and out pops the little bird, as though eager to pick one of the cards spread across the table and determine your destiny. Once it chooses your fate, the old man regards the card solemnly to tell you what it means. Sometimes, that isn't enough; then he has you extend your palm toward him, sprinkles baby powder on it—the better to see the lines—and lets you know what your future holds. We've seen grown men shed tears, young girls blush, and elegant old ladies stalk away in anger from the fortune-teller's table; such is his power.

I wonder sometimes what he would see in my palm. I wonder if I even want to know.

"Such a wise old bird," Saf whispers, interrupting my thoughts. An elderly gentleman in a sarong and songkok takes his seat in front of the fortune-teller's table, his back ramrod straight. He nods, and the fortune-teller taps the cage. On cue, the parrot hops out and makes its way to the cards spread across the table, its head tilted to one side inquiringly. "The parrot or the uncle?" I quip, and we giggle as we eagerly accept small steel bowls of the sweet, chilled liquid, generously filled with juicy longan, dried winter melon, and monk fruit.

"Did you see the parade last night?" Refreshed, palms tingling from the ice-cold bowls, we saunter on down the street, past a row of trishaw drivers snoozing in the shade while waiting for passengers.

"Heard them, more like." Mama chokes on a bite of her tiffin lunch and falls to the ground writhing and gasping for breath, her face a mottled purple blue, and I reach up, ostensibly to smooth back a hair that's escaped from the braid that hangs down my back, but really to tap quickly three times on each side of my head. *That's better*, the Djinn coos. "Mama wouldn't let me go outside to take a look. Said they were just being hooligans, overexcited after winning some election seats." I care little about politics—it seems to me like it's mostly a bunch of old men competing to see who has the loudest voice—but just days before, the government's Alliance Party had won less than half of the popular vote for the first time ever, and the two new Chinese parties had won victories nobody had expected. The aftershocks from this had shaken our neighborhood to its core, and everyone was still talking about it.

"What did you hear?" Saf is wide-eyed with excitement. "Was it really bad? Norma said they were waving

red flags and posters with Mao Zedong's face on them!
She said they were throwing pig flesh at people's houses
and spitting on the doors all the way through Kampung
Baru!" She shudders at the thrill and taboo of it all. Our
neighborhood is the largest Malay enclave in the city, and
pig flesh is the ultimate insult for devout Muslim Malays,
who view pigs not just as meat we're forbidden from eating, but as the dirtiest of animals, unholy, unclean.

I roll my eyes. "Norma is such a drama queen. I don't
think they were doing any of that. At least, I didn't see any
pig bits at our door this morning. . . ."

"My father says they should be shot. He says all it
took was their party winning a few parliamentary seats
for them to forget how to be grateful, that they need to
remember this is Tanah Melayu, the land of the Malays.
He says they're nothing but troublemakers and Communists."

I shrug. "Your father thinks everyone's a troublemaker
or Communist."

"That's true." Saf's father is a teacher at one of the
boys' schools in town, where he is notorious for being
stingy with his praise and generous with his cane. Whenever Saf leaves the house, he forces her to stand perfectly
straight, hands at her sides, for the fingertip test: Unless the
hem of the skirt comes well past the tips of her fingers, she
isn't allowed to take a single step out the door. Not without

reason; Saf's dimpled sweetness—and as we got older, the way her uniform skimmed over her gentle curves—have always called to the boys like sugar to an anthill. Though she professes innocence, Saf is a notorious flirt. "You girls behave yourselves," he tells us sternly whenever we go out. "No gadding about, and mind you get home before the azan." The mosque's call to prayer that echoes through the village each sunset has been our cue to head home for as long as I can remember.

"So it was just a parade? Nothing serious?"

"I guess not. But . . ."

"But what?"

"I mean . . . I didn't understand all of it. There was a lot of singing, a lot of chanting. They were yelling things in Chinese, saying we should go back to the jungle, that we should leave now that the country is theirs. I know someone was shouting that Malays should . . . should go and die." I close my eyes briefly, remembering the roar of the lorry engines, the banging of the drums, the shouting, the accompanying wave of nausea and fear. We're no strangers to violence in Kampung Baru; once every few weeks, Mama locks the doors and windows as the sounds of neighborhood gangs battling full tilt filter through our home's wooden slats. But those are run-of-the-mill turf wars, arrogant Malay boys duking it out for control of the neighborhood. This felt bigger, somehow, and dangerous.

As if on cue, the Djinn clicks another movie reel into place: Mama, beaten with iron pipes and run through with sharpened sticks, her head nothing more than a mass of bloody pulp. I shake my head and resist the urge to count all the rambutans piled in woven baskets at a nearby stall. *Go away*, I tell him. *Go away.*

"Are you okay?" My eyes fly open. Saf is staring at me, brows furrowed with concern.

I feel a sudden urge to tell her, to blurt out everything, all at once. *No, Saf, I'm not okay. I haven't been okay for a long time now. I'm constantly imagining my own mother's death. I spend all my time and energy wrestling with a demon in my head that only I can see or hear, and anytime I'm not doing that, I'm busy counting and tapping everything in sight just to shut him up. I'm really, really not okay. I'm so far from okay I don't even remember what okay feels like anymore.*

Yeah right.

"I'm fine," I say quickly. "Just daydreaming. So, um, what records shall we look at today?"

We tried to pretend at first that what was wrong with me could easily be fixed. Mama took me to a doctor, where I skated lightly over my visions and concentrated heavily on my inability to fall asleep at night and the way thoughts raced through my head, impossible to capture and examine one by one; he tapped his pen against his chin thoughtfully and prescribed iron pills, a more balanced diet, and exercise.

"You need to stay active," he told me sternly. "Some strenuous activity will tire you out, help you sleep better at night, help you not think so much about things." He clicked his tongue as he wrote on his notepad in loopy, illegible handwriting. "You young people, life is so easy for you. No job yet, no families to raise, no responsibilities. I don't know what you think you have to worry about." On the way home we stopped at the shops, where my mother bought more fruits and vegetables than the two of us could possibly eat, badminton rackets, and a can of shuttlecocks. "This will be fun!" she says gaily, and I nod glumly. *Sure. Fun.*

And so we went for a while, our meals greener than ever, our evenings spent gamely sending the shuttlecock flying over the gate, which acted as a makeshift net. Sometimes Saf would come over for a game. I even had fun, most of the time, except that through the chatter and the laughter, I was obsessively counting each *thwack* as racket hit shuttlecock, back and forth, over and over again. Everyone thought I was extraordinarily competitive; they didn't realize that I was desperate to get to twenty-one, a nice, safe number that just so happened to mean that I also won. Badminton made the Djinn inordinately happy.

It didn't take long to realize that it wasn't working. The badminton stopped the day I lost a game to Mama, fourteen to twenty-one, and spent the next twenty minutes tapping my racket on the ground on my left, then right, three times each, over and over again, because fourteen can't be divided by three and nothing in the world felt right anymore. That was the day I smashed my racket on the ground and dissolved into a red-faced mass of frustration and tears, and Mama locked the remaining racket and the can of shuttlecocks away in a cupboard somewhere.

Sure, I was eating better and exercising more, but all that meant was that I was a marginally healthier bundle of teeming, frayed nerves than I was before. The visions didn't stop, the voice that intruded in my thoughts didn't stop, and the urgent need to count things certainly didn't stop.

In the wee hours of a Sunday morning, when I should have been asleep but was really tangled in a complicated ritual that involved pacing my room in specific patterns, tapping certain objects three times as I passed, all to make sure that my mother would wake up in the morning, I heard a strangled sob through the thin walls and froze.

Mama?

I pressed my right ear against the wall that divides my room from the kitchen, trying to ignore the instant, indignant buzzing that demanded I finish pacing. Why was Mama crying?

"I don't know what to do," she was saying through her sobs, presumably to my Mak Su, my youngest aunt, who had slept over the night before. "She's changed so completely. It's like her body's been taken over by a complete stranger. It looks like her, but acts nothing like her."

My heart hammered so loud I was almost sure she could hear me.

I could hear Mak Su's voice, low and soothing. I imagined her holding Mama close, rubbing her back in little circles.

"What about the specialist?" she asked. "You know, the one at the hospital. The mental doctor." She lingered over the last three words, and fresh panic bloomed in my chest.

"Absolutely not." Mama was firm. "Those quacks will just send her to the asylum, or worse. I hear they cut up people's brains, trying to fix them. Nobody's doing that to Melati."

A pause. Then Mak Su's reedy voice piped up. "We've seen this happen before—you know, in the village," she said in hushed tones, and I strained to hear her. "They say it's the work of djinns."

"Are you serious?" Mama was high-pitched, disbelieving. She's never been one for superstition; when Saf and I came home bearing tales of fortune-tellers, lucky charms, witch doctors, and love potions, she would scoff, telling us that only fools put their faith in magic instead of themselves. "We make our own luck in this world, girls," she'd say.

In the kitchen, Mak Su was defensive. "No, it's true! They possess her, force her to act strangely. Maybe someone's cursed your family. . . . Do you know if anyone holds a grudge against you?"

Curses? Djinns? It was the sort of thing that appeared in swashbuckling adventure stories; Sinbad, perhaps, or the *Tales from the Thousand and One Nights*. In a life so devoid of either swash or buckle, how could I, of all people, have ended up with a djinn?

The thoughts swirling around my head were making me dizzy. I reached out a hand to steady myself and accidentally pushed over a little pile of books neatly arranged on my desk, largest at the bottom, smallest at the top, and spines perfectly aligned. They toppled over with a *crash* that seemed even louder in the predawn hush. "Shhh," I heard my mother hiss, then loudly, "Melati? Is that you?"

I'd come out of my room then, rubbing my eyes and pretending I'd heard nothing. We drank hot tea and Mak Su made lempeng pisang, the banana pancakes sweet and sticky and burning our fingers as we ate them fresh off the pan, and we talked as if nothing had happened and the world hadn't just shifted.

But it had, because now I knew.

The Djinn lives inside me, and he feeds on my rituals. As long as I meet his demands, he'll keep my mother safe. When I try to resist, frustrated at being in constant thrall to the numbers, he sets off another chain of deaths in my head, then laughs at my horrified reaction. The beast must be fed, and for a year now, I've alternated between feeding him and wrestling him into silence.

I'm so tired.

The shop on the corner seems to have been there since the dawn of time, though I know for a fact that it's been there for more than ten years now. Records occupy almost every available inch of space; what doesn't fit in the rows of shelves ends up piled high on tables, stools, and various other surfaces, all arranged in a haphazard system that only the aged proprietor seems to know. Music spills out from its tiny confines onto the streets, anything from traditional Chinese operettas to the latest Pop Yeh Yeh numbers; Uncle has eclectic tastes. Today, the Beatles wail encouragement to passersby, assuring them that their girl still loves them. "She knows you're not the hurting kind," they say. I take this as a good omen.

"You girls again," he grumbles when he sees us.

"Hello Uncle!" we chorus. "Aren't you happy to see us?" Saf smiles at him winningly.

"Ya, ya, you two. Play the records only, chatter, chatter, chatter, block the aisles, then never buy." He sniffs disapprovingly.

"We don't have that much money lah Uncle," says Saf.

"You got the new Shadows EP, Uncle?" I ask, flipping through the sleeves and sneezing at the dust I dislodge in the process.

He grunts. "Of course lah I got." Before long, we're immersed in records new and old, swaying and dancing, mouthing along to the plaintive *yeah-yeah-yeah*s and nodding our heads as we browse the aisles. But just when I feel myself start to relax, the Djinn catches me off guard with a particularly gruesome image of Mama's limp, lifeless body, one that feels like a punch to the stomach.

Count for me, Melati, he whispers softly in my ear. *Count.*

No, I tell him fiercely. *Stop it.* I stride purposefully over to the corner where the Uncle's record player sits on its own special table and wrench at the volume knob until the music is blaring so loudly that I can feel the floorboards shake. Saf shrieks with laughter at this uncharacteristic act of rebellion, and Uncle yells, "Aiya, aiya, you will deafen me lah girl!" And the Beatles tell me that I should be glad, and I am, because at last, I don't hear the Djinn at all.

Before the movie, we make one more stop at the vendors lined up across the street. I get us kuaci and boiled nuts to share, each twisted neatly into a white paper cone. Saf uses the time I spend purchasing them to flirt shamelessly with Jason, who blushes and dips his head shyly in response as he mans his father's sugarcane stall. Then, giggling, we head for the Rex, its walls plastered with hand-painted posters emblazoned with the impossibly beautiful faces of the stars du jour. PAUL NEWMAN IN A HELL-OF-A-RACING-STORY! they scream in black on lurid red. PAUL NEWMAN IN A HELL-OF-A-ROMANCE!

Clutching our second-class tickets, we head into the hall and look for our seats, casting envious glances at those making their way up the stairs to the highly coveted first-class section. With each step, I can feel my feet peel slowly off the floor, sticky with layers of spilled drinks and spit, and littered with dozens of white kuaci shells that crunch beneath our feet.

"Don't sit there," Saf whispers, pointing to a lone seat covered in bright red cloth and surrounded by empty chairs. "They say that one's haunted." I roll my eyes—sure it is—but when we pass I find myself giving it a wide berth anyway; one vengeful spirit at a time is enough for me.

As the lights dim and the roar of racing engines begins to fill the air, Mama slips in the darkness and breaks her neck with a sickening *snap*, her body lying limp, limbs akimbo like the rag doll I used to cuddle to sleep.

There is no music to save me this time.

I lean back, close my eyes, and tap my middle fingers on my knees: three times on the right, three times on the left, then back again, and again, and again. I do that forty-two times, until the picture goes away and I can finally concentrate on Paul Newman's hell-of-a-racing-story.

"I have to watch it again," Saf says. "I just have to." She sighs, leaning back in her seat. "Oh, Paul. Why is he so perfect?"

I laugh. "You're not serious."

"I am, actually. Right now!"

"Saf, no! You're going to burn through all your pocket money!"

"For Paul," she says, smiling that dimpled smile, her eyes shining with excitement. "Paul is worth it."

"You're cuckoo." I shake my head. "I'm heading home."

"Come on, Mel. . . ."

"No way," I tell her. "Once was enough for me." And I mean it, though it has nothing to do with how I feel about Paul and his blue eyes, and everything to do with how very, very tired I am with this hidden battle for my own thoughts, the burden of counting, the work it takes to hide it. The Djinn hates it when I'm adrift in the world, trying to live my life; he prefers me anchored to my home, where I can feed his need for numbers without fear of discovery.

"Suit yourself." Saf jumps up and heads to the lobby. "I'm going to go get another ticket!"

I follow along behind her and make my way outside, waving to her as I go. I have to smile at Saf's exuberance, her determination to squeeze the joy out of every moment, her willingness to hurtle through life by the seat of her pants. From where I stand, enmeshed in a cage of numbers and secrets, it looks a lot like freedom.

It takes two steps out the door for the smile to fade.

Something is wrong. Something is very, very wrong.

Petaling Street is deserted.

Where the bustling, heaving, vibrant crowd was mere hours before, there is silence. The shops are shuttered, the vendors have disappeared, leaving only the usual marketplace debris behind them—here, a crumpled paper bag, still bearing traces of its greasy occupants; there, a small pile of sugarcane husks, squeezed dry of their sweet juice. Where the fortune-teller was, a handful of white cards lie scattered on the grubby pavement: remnants of other people's fortunes. Twilight bathes everything in a curious, eerie light, making it look as if I've stepped into another realm.

The Djinn twirls his clawed fingers, shooting delicate tendrils of icy-cold fear into my chest.

A lone trishaw driver cycles by, panting hard, his legs pumping like pistons, his pointed hat knocked askew.

"Uncle, Uncle," I call after him. "Where is everyone? What's going on?"

He pauses and looks back, taking in my turquoise school pinafore, the half-filled cone of kuaci still in my hand. "Go home, girl," he says. "Go home. It's not safe here."

Safe. I feel it then: the familiar tightening in my throat; the cold sweat trickling down my forehead and forging trails down my neck. "Why, Uncle? What's happening?"

He pauses. "They're killing one another," he says finally. "The Malays and the Chinese are killing one another."

Then he looks away and cycles off, as hard and as fast as he can, until he turns the corner and disappears altogether. The crumpled paper cone drops from my hand, and white kuaci shells scatter on the sidewalk.

CHAPTER THREE

THE MALAYS AND CHINESE ARE killing one another.

They're killing one another.

Killing.

Killing.

KILLING.

The word crashes around my head. My breath comes in shallow pants, and the Djinn is screaming: *They're coming for her. They're coming for her. They're going to kill Mama, Melati—they'll kill her and you'll have nobody left.*

The numbers, I think, *the numbers. One, two, three. One, two, three. That's it. One, two, three. Breathe.* The numbers buy me some time, quell the beast momentarily, shut down the images jostling around screaming for my attention, each more graphic and painful than the last, and all of them featuring Mama.

Saf. I have to get Saf. We have to get out of here. I turn

on my heels and sprint back into the Rex, making straight for the theater doors, counting each step.

"Excuse me! Excuse me, miss!"

"What?" I turn, breathing hard, my mind so full of numbers I can barely see straight. "What? What is it?"

The gangly youth in the red usher's uniform looks at me sternly over the top of his spectacles. "You have a ticket, miss?"

"A ticket?" *Three, six, nine, twelve, fifteen, eighteen . . . This isn't going to be enough*, I think, and I slide my right hand into my skirt pocket and tap my fingers quickly in time to the beat.

"Yes, a ticket. For the movie. No admittance without a ticket."

A ticket? Is this guy serious right now?

"It's an emergency! I have to get my friend. There's—"

"No. Admittance. Without. A. Ticket." He says it slowly and deliberately, emphasizing each word, as though I am hard of hearing, or hard of thinking, or both.

I grit my teeth and think about how satisfying it would feel to punch him. "Fine," I say, throwing my hands up and heading for the ticket office. "Fine, I'll go and buy another ticket."

Minutes later I'm back at the door, ticket in hand, and the usher, now puffy with self-importance at having completed his task, makes a grand show of examining it carefully and tearing the stub before opening the door with a flourish. Inside, the theater is already dark, and he walks before me, shining his flashlight along the rows until at last, we spot Saf right in the center of the hall, staring at the screen in rapt attention. I quickly begin to work my way toward her. "Sorry, sorry, excuse me, sorry," I murmur, banging into all number of shins and knees and counting seats furiously inside my head until at last I manage to squeeze into the one beside Saf (number fifteen—a good sign).

"Saf!" I hiss.

"Hmm? Oh, hi!" Saf grins at me. "Couldn't resist, huh? I don't blame you—it's so good."

"Uh-huh." I jab her in the ribs. "Come on, we have to go."

"What?"

"We have to go."

Saf stares at me, bewildered. "Why would we do that?" she says. "The movie isn't even over."

Paul Newman has just won his race. From the recesses behind us comes a loud, distinct "SHHHHH." In the glow of the movie screen, I can just make out the disapproving faces of the couple in the next row, glaring at us. I tug desperately at Saf's sleeve. "Come on, Saf, come on, please. Please."

You're running out of time, the Djinn says helpfully.

Ticktock, ticktock. He pounds to the beat on the inside of my chest, and my school blouse is suddenly about five sizes too small, and I can't breathe, and we have. To. Get. Out. Of. Here.

"Can you two please keep it down?" The male half of the disapproving couple can no longer contain his impatience. "We are paying customers, you know—we have rights!"

"Come on, Saf, come on, come on, come on. . . ."

Saf sighs. "Okay, fine, you weirdo. Let's go."

As we make our way out of the row—"Finally," a voice behind us mutters—I feel a relief so palpable it almost makes my knees buckle. Now we can go home, and Mama will make everything right.

Suddenly, just as Paul Newman stoically receives a kiss on the cheek from a blond beauty queen, the movie stutters to a stop, and the screen goes blank. Outraged voices chime up in the darkness: "What's the big idea?" "Is it broken?" "Fix the movie; we want to know what happens next!"

Nothing happens.

Then suddenly, the screen blinks back to life. Against a bright red background, stark black letters blink the same message over and over again: EMERGENCY DECLARED.

The lights come back on, flooding the room, leaving us all blinking at the brightness.

The Djinn perks up then, alert, anticipating. An immediate sense of deep, deep dread settles in the pit of my stomach. The room buzzes with panicky energy as everyone begins to get up and head for the exit. "Come on," I say, dragging Saf by the sleeve. "We have to go. . . ."

The words die on my lips.

The men stand silently in front of the theater doors, blocking the exits. Some wield parangs, their cold steel glinting in the dim glow of the screen; some hold iron pipes; some bear large wooden sticks, hacked to sharp, deadly points. Several boast scars and tattoos that peek out from beneath their rolled-up sleeves, marking them as members of the same gang.

One, clearly the leader, steps forward. "Ladies and gentlemen," he booms in accented Malay, his voice echoing through the room. "Sorry to interrupt your show. There's been . . . a change of plans." He smiles, revealing rows of perfectly even, white teeth. "I'm going to need all the Malays to stand over here"—he gestures to his right, the blade of the sharp knife he grips glinting in the light— "and all you other fellas to stand over there." The knife whips around as he gestures to his left.

There is a moment when everything seems to freeze, when everyone looks at each other, unsure what to do next.

"I suggest you move quickly," the man says quietly. He isn't smiling anymore.

There is a great rustling then, as people jostle to do as he says. My head is a symphony of a thousand deaths, and I bite back the urge to count every single seat in the theater until my brain shuts up or shuts down, whichever comes first. "We have to try and get out," I whisper to Saf, who is visibly pale and shaking imperceptibly. "We have to—"

"You."

The man is in front of us now. Beside me, I feel Saf freeze, and before I even realize it, I shift my body so that it's ever so slightly in front of hers. The Djinn howls, flitting from my stomach to my chest and back again, sending my insides roiling.

The man eyes Saf, with her clear brown skin, her heavy brows. "Melayu. Over there." He reaches past me and shoves her roughly toward the rest of the Malays on the right, and a whimper escapes as she makes her way to the group, not daring to disobey. He turns to me next, and I shiver slightly at the look in his eyes. It's not the hostility that's disconcerting—it's the glint buried behind it, the little spark that shows how much he's enjoying this.

"Now you," he says to me, taking in my light skin, my eyes, my face. "Melayu atau Cina?" I know I should answer, but I can't think, can't speak over the noise in my head.

He smacks me on the side of my head, none too gently. "Oi. You deaf? Melayu atau Cina?"

"Eurasian."

The voice is loud, older, and it rings out from the non-Malay half of the theater.

"Hah?" The man turns; I turn; the entire auditorium turns to see where it's coming from.

"She's Eurasian." The speaker is a Chinese lady in her midfifties, her dark hair pulled back into a neat bun, her elegant blue cheongsam scattered with tiny pink flowers. She walks calmly toward us. "You know. Eurasian. Serani. She's one of my neighbors' girls. We live near Petaling Jaya."

The man snorts disbelievingly. "Then why can't she tell me so herself? No voice? Or no brain?"

"Can't you see how frightened she is? You think it's easy to talk to you?" She sniffs. "I see your face; I also would be scared to talk to you."

There is a pause, and the man seems to think this over, staring at the auntie, who meets his gaze unflinchingly. Then he shrugs. "Fine, Auntie, you win. Take her home." He turns to the Chinese and Indian moviegoers. "In fact, you can all go. Bye-bye. Have a nice night."

The non-Malays quickly file toward the exits, none of them daring to look at the desperate faces of those they leave behind. The soft sounds of sobbing waft over from the huddled Malays—twelve in all.

I can't do it. I can't go. I can't leave Saf.

"What about them?" I say loudly, trying to keep the tremor from my voice. "What will happen to them?"

Silence. Everyone seems to freeze. Then the sounds of harsh laughter. "Only what they deserve, girl," the man tells me, smiling that vicious smile.

The auntie jabs me in the small of my back. "Come, girl, I take you home, come."

"No!" I squirm at her touch, looking desperately back at Saf. "I can't leave her! I can't leave my friend!" A hand lands gently on my shoulder as the auntie leans forward to whisper in my ear. "Girl," she says, "it's no good staying, it will mean you both die instead of just one. Listen, please, come with me." The hand drags me away, steering my reluctant feet to the door.

The men begin to move toward the little group then, with all the menacing grace of hunters stalking their prey. I can taste the salt of my own tears on my lips. *I'm sorry*, I mouth over and over again. *I'm sorry, I'm sorry, I'm so, so sorry.*

The last thing I see as I turn back is Saf's pale, frightened face, her eyes huge with despair and unshed tears, her hand outstretched in mute appeal.

Then the doors close, and there is nothing but the heavy weight of oppressive silence.

CHAPTER FOUR

I CAN'T BREATHE.

I'm on my knees, gulping air, a million pinpricks of pain shooting through my arms and legs. Spots dance in intricate patterns in front of my eyes, and my thoughts are racing so fast I don't feel like I can ever keep up. From far, far away, through the fog of pain and panic, I can hear a voice: "Are you all right? Girl, are you all right?" A hand on my shoulder, shaking me gently, then harder, then harder still. "Aiya, girl, get up, get up!"

"I can't breathe," I manage to choke out. "I can't breathe." The Djinn has me in a viselike grip, his arms like steel bands squeezing against my ribs, forcing the air out of my lungs. The street echoes with my rasping and wheezing. Through the dancing spots I can just make out the auntie's kindly face hovering beside me.

"You can," she says simply. "Just take your time. I wait here with you." And she sits next to me primly in her fitted blue dress, for all the world as if we're waiting for tea to be served.

Tap your fingers three times on your right knee, three times on your left, three times with your right foot, three times with your left. Again. Three times right knee, three times left . . .

It takes thirty-three sets of this for me to feel right again, except Saf is gone and nothing will ever feel right again, ever. I am shaky and exhausted and want nothing more than to evaporate into tears and nothingness.

"Are you finished?"

I jump; I've been so focused on the numbers that I'd honestly forgotten she was even there. "Um. Yes?"

Did she see me? Has she been watching me this entire time? I can feel an ugly hot flush creeping across my face and down my neck. *You're not supposed to be seen. You're never supposed to be seen.*

I've gotten used to keeping my little quirks hidden. I'm pretty smart anyway, but it doesn't take a genius to realize that to be inflicted with djinns ranks right up there as among the worst things that can happen to you when you're sixteen years old and studying in an all-girls' school. Girls are vicious creatures. You could tie your hair wrong one day and be ostracized by your friends the next. Your mother could come to school dressed in an embarrassing outfit one morning and by that afternoon you could be the butt of jokes for the entire school. To be different is to be mocked mercilessly. Be unique at your own peril.

Every day for me is like its own special, specific challenge: find ways to appease the Djinn and his voracious appetite for numbers, without letting anyone realize that I'm doing it. Finger- and toe-tapping is easy enough to explain away—*Oh, that lesson was so boring, I had to move around to keep myself from falling asleep!* Sometimes I get too engrossed in getting the numbers right; *Oh, just daydreaming,* I say, dropping some hints about a boy and smiling mysteriously, letting everyone assume I'm another silly girl getting starry-eyed over the opposite sex. I tap my tongue with my teeth, blink my eyes in sync with my counting, chant numbers in my head, count words in textbooks, tap with my fingers hidden in my pocket or with my toes encased safely in my canvas school shoes. Safe. Nobody ever has to find out my secret.

But here's this kindly-faced older woman, staring directly at me and seemingly unfazed by the bizarre barrage of tapping and twitching she's just witnessed.

"Yes, Auntie," I say again, cautiously. "I'm finished." *She thinks you're crazy,* the Djinn whispers, sending tiny tentacles of doubt to wrap themselves around my brain. I shake my head quickly, trying to dislodge them.

"Good, good. Can you talk or not?"

"Can, Auntie." *Look at her. Look at the way she's eyeing you. Like you're a wild animal.*

"Okay. You have a name?"

"Melati, Auntie." *She hates you for abandoning your friend, you know. She knows it's your fault Saf was killed.*

I can feel myself start to panic. Quickly, I blink, three times in rapid succession, then again, then again.

Again. Until you get it right.

"Okay, Melati. You can call me Auntie Bee." She hoists herself back up with a slight grimace, dusting off her knees. "You'd better come home with me first. It's getting dark, and it's not safe for you to be out here."

Look at you. You can't even save yourself. And you think you can save your mother? His laughter grates on me like nails dragged across a chalkboard.

I pause ever so slightly before nodding three times— one, two, three. I've been given all the talks about going places with strangers, and she's Chinese, which, based on recent experience, means there's about a 50 percent chance that she wants to kill me. But considering she just saved my butt for no good reason, stabbing me out here in the streets probably isn't the highest thing on her to-do list. I don't see any other alternative; the Djinn weighs heavily on my stooped shoulders, I'm tired, and frankly, Auntie Bee isn't going to take no for an answer. I can tell. It's the primal law of auntie-hood: No matter whether Chinese, Malay, or

Indian, an auntie can just say something and assume everyone will rearrange themselves to obey, and so strong is this belief in their own rightness that people usually do.

The older woman sighs, looking up and down the empty streets. "How are we going to do this?" she mutters to herself, frowning. Then a jab on my arm. "Come, girl," she says. "We'd better walk. Maybe we'll see a car or a bus, somebody who can take us home."

I stagger onto my feet and allow myself to be dragged by the arm up Petaling Street. Not a sound disturbs the strange quiet all around us, but beneath this veneer of silence, the Djinn cackles gleefully and brings up image after image of Mama's death, feeding on the charged atmosphere around us: a buzzing undercurrent of thick tension, a sense that there is more to come.

Then, as I count feverishly in my head, it comes.

"What is that?" Auntie Bee frowns, craning her neck to see ahead of us.

Down the road they come, dozens of them, brandishing knives and sticks, the strips of bright red cloth tied around their waists and heads trailing merrily behind them, flapping in the breeze. "Allahu akbar!" they yell. "Allahu akbar!" And for a moment I am struck by how strange it is to proclaim the greatness of God, a phrase we say over and over again in prayer five times a day, while doing their best to destroy His creations.

"Run, girl, run!" Auntie Bee's shouts break through my reverie and we dash as fast as we can down the street. I have no time to stop, no time to think, no time to count, no time to breathe. I'm not that athletic on the best of days—my PE teacher once wrote a note home to my mother that included the lines "barely able to exert herself for five minutes" and "constantly trying to be excused on the basis of 'period pain,' which would be possible only if she had three periods every month"—and it doesn't take long for me to be gasping for breath, a burning pain radiating from my lungs. I glance to my left; Auntie Bee is doing no better, her face bright red with the effort, but she keeps a firm grip on my arm and hurries me along. Behind us, I hear the sounds of shouting and smashing glass.

"Come on, come on," she puffs. "We must keep moving." Her eyes constantly scan our surroundings for possible hiding places; she knows we can't run forever.

When we turn the corner, I see him: an older man, his brown face worn from the beating of the years and the sun, his mustache and hair peppered with gray. "Here, here!" he says, beckoning wildly to us, and in the absence of any other options, Auntie Bee and I slow down. I can sense her hesitation with each step that brings us closer to him. I can't really blame her. Malay men are busy burning down Petaling Street; there's no real way of knowing if this particular Malay man can be trusted.

"Quickly," he says. "Come quickly." And he gestures behind him, where I now notice a large drain, partially covered with metal sheeting and blocked from view by a trishaw—*his* trishaw. "Go in there," he says, pointing at the drain. "There's still space. Hurry."

I look over at Auntie Bee, who nods quickly and grasps the man's hand in a gesture of unspoken gratitude as we pass. Then we scurry to the drain and I jump into the dark cavern, landing on my feet with a sickening *squelch*. The floor of the drain is wet and yields slightly beneath my weight, and I try very hard not to think about the reasons why while Auntie Bee lowers herself more cautiously, grunting with the effort. Inside, there are already two others, but beyond the fact that they're a man and woman, there's little else I can see in the darkness to identify them. The air is heavy with the scent of sweat and rancid drain water, and I have to concentrate on taking deep, even breaths without throwing up. Through a small hole in the sheeting that covers us, I see the man reposition his trishaw slightly to better hide us from view. His body is tense, muscles tightly coiled as a cat ready to spring. The hands that grip the handlebars tremble slightly.

We wait.

I freeze, trying to make myself as still and as small as possible, trying to quiet my heart, which is beating so loudly I'm sure its rhythmic tattoo echoes down the streets. Auntie Bee's lips move in silent prayer, and I add my own, tapping manically with my fingers: *Onetwo-threeonetwothreeonetwothreeonetwothree*, the words blurring together until they don't even make sense.

Then we hear it. The roar of the mob gets closer, louder. I suddenly smell the acrid scent of smoke. From beside me, a sharp intake of breath from Auntie Bee. "They're burning the shops," she mutters. "They're burning the shops." There is a loud clattering of footsteps running frantically past us where we crouch hidden from sight; in the distance, I hear an anguished cry. I start to shiver and can't seem to make myself stop. From my peephole, I realize the man has picked up a stick from his trishaw. "Allahu akbar!" he yells along with the crowd, his fist raised. "Allahu akbar!" They sweep past him, smashing windows, setting fire to abandoned cars. It is wild and raucous and terrifying.

Then suddenly, a car appears—a blue Morris Minor—and screeches to a stop down the road, just within view. The door opens and a man darts out. "Come, come, quickly," he calls, waving at those running desperately from the riot, his dark skin glistening with sweat. For a moment, my heart lifts crazily. *There's a car! He can save them!*

It doesn't take long for my hopes to be dashed. Before anyone can even make it into the car, the red bands turn to him. The man with the blue Morris Minor immediately backs away, his hands in the air. "Indian scum!" someone yells. "Don't let him get away!"

"Please, I mean no harm," the would-be savior says, inching his way back to the car, his hands still stretched toward the sky. "Just let me go. I mean no harm."

It does no good. Before he can say any more, his car is suddenly aflame, and he steps away from it with a shocked cry. He doesn't get very far. The mob descends. There are *thud*s and *thwack*s and a heart-thumping *crunch* as the flying fists connect with his various body parts, until finally, bruised and bloodied, he is pushed hard in the chest, so hard that he goes flying into the flames.

I close my eyes and turn away, but even though I count and count and count and count, there is nothing I can do to stop his agonized screams from ringing in my head long after the men have moved on and there is nothing but silence on the streets.

Eventually, the trishaw man, gray-faced and trembling, comes back to our hiding place and helps us clamber out: Auntie Bee and me, a young Chinese man who immediately sprints away down the street, and a pretty Indian girl who can't stop thanking him through her tears as she stumbles away.

"I am so sorry," he says to us, shaking his head. "I wish I could take you where you need to go, but I don't

DAVA, JANISE EMILY

think it's safe. If the Chinese see me, I'm dead. And if the Malays see me with Chinese in my trishaw, I'm dead." I can see that he means it, and so can Auntie Bee. "You've done more than enough," she says gently. "Thank you."

Auntie Bee coaxes me, with a tremor in her voice that she can't quite mask, to keep walking, but my brain won't stop counting and the Djinn won't stop screaming in my ears and I can't quite make my legs move the way I want them to. She's trying her best not to nag me, to keep encouraging me, but I can see from the way she's jiggling her foot with each pause that I'm holding her back. "You should go, Auntie," I gasp the third time we stop. "You should go ahead. I'm sure I'll be fine on my own."

"Don't be silly, girl."

In the distance, we hear the crash of breaking glass, then yells and cheers. Auntie Bee clicks her tongue, looking up and down the street. Then she nods firmly to herself and snaps to attention. "Right," she says. "You can't move fast, and we can't stay out here, so our only option is to stay hidden until they're properly gone. Right?"

"Right."

"All right. There's a shop down there that doesn't have its shutters down; the owner must have run off when all the troubles started. We'll slip inside and stay out of harm's way. Come."

She offers me an arm to lean on, and together we make

our way to the little shop. It's too dark to make out what the sign above the door says, but when we enter I'm hit by the smooth, rich smell of fine leather. Auntie Bee tugs at me to follow her. "I don't want to risk turning on the light," she says as we fumble our way through the darkness. I bang my knee against something—a low table?—and bite back an agonized moan.

We crouch down behind a counter piled high with leather skins to wait it out. In the silence, I tap softly against the cold stone floor.

The yells are getting closer and closer, and beside me, I feel Auntie Bee shiver. Neither of us says a word.

Then, suddenly, we hear it. "This one!" a harsh voice yells from right outside.

Then a crash as glass breaks and splinters.

Then a *whoosh*, and a rush of heat.

Fire.

For a second, all we can do is stare at each other in the sudden brightness as the flames spread to lick the wooden cabinets, stools, and tables strewn about the shop.

Then she grabs my hand and we run, stumbling in our haste to get away from the flames that leap and dance between us and the door. Auntie Bee makes a beeline for a window toward the back of the shop, and I follow, covering my mouth to keep from choking on the thick smoke. "Hurry!" I tell her frantically, but when she finally prizes the shutter open, wrought-iron bars block the opening.

The Djinn fills my veins with icy panic and, combined with the creeping heat, my entire body trembles uncontrollably.

"There must be another door," she says, running into the back room. I follow, fighting the urge to curl up and let the flames take me.

There is a back door, and it's locked. "Come and help me," Auntie Bee says, and together we launch ourselves at it, trying to force it open with our combined weight. The door shudders but stays steadfastly closed. The Djinn laughs, running a clawed finger up my spine.

"Again," Auntie Bee says, her jaw set. "Come on."

Again and again, we throw our shoulders against the door. Behind us, I hear the *crack* of the flames consuming everything in their path. "Don't look," Auntie Bee says. "Concentrate."

On the fifth try, the door finally flies open, and we spill out into the tiny back alley that stretches behind the row of shophouses. I suck in the cool night air greedily, filling my lungs until I think they may collapse. Beside me, Auntie Bee is bent over, heaving, her body wracked with dry retches that yield no vomit, but still look like they hurt like hell.

Eventually, we recover enough to straighten up and dust the grime from our clothes.

"Come on," Auntie Bee says. "We have to get out of here." As we stumble back toward the now-deserted main road, her arm over my shoulder as though to shore me up, a little gray Standard comes tearing up the road and comes to a dead stop right in front of us. Auntie Bee's face relaxes into a smile. "Vincent! You came for me!"

The young man in the driver's seat is tall and thin, with legs so long that his knees jam against the steering wheel in a way that looks decidedly uncomfortable. "Of course, Ma. Baba told me you were at the theater as usual, and when we heard about the troubles, I thought I'd better come get you. Are you all right? Are you hurt? I saw the fire. . . ." His eyes slide over to me, pale and crumpled beside his mother, and he stops abruptly. "Who's this?"

She's already dragging me to the car. "This is Melati. She's coming with us."

"But, Ma, why are we taking her with us? Where's her family? Won't they worry about her?" Vincent runs a hand through his dark hair, which flops into his eyes, and which Saf's dad would probably harrumph at as being a shade too long to be a "proper man's haircut," adding a grumble about "those damned dandies" for good measure. His expression is half-angry, half-confused. "I really don't think this is a good idea. No offense," he adds, flicking his eyes in my direction.

"None taken," I mumble back, too busy counting the

pebbles on the ground so that I can ignore the sharp pang that pierced my stomach the moment Saf's name wafted through my mind. I can't blame him anyway. Who wants some strange girl in their car, especially one that looks as though she might throw up at any moment?

Auntie Bee waves her hand at him, as only a true auntie can. "Stop your nonsense, please, Vincent. She needs somewhere to go, and we're taking her with us. End of story." Having successfully deposited me, pliant and unprotesting, into the back seat, she slams the door shut and slides into the passenger seat beside her son. "What is this?" she asks, gesturing to the windshield, where a crack snakes from the right-hand side all the way to the left, blossoming from a hole almost perfectly centered over the driver's seat.

"Nothing," Vincent says, shrugging. "Just some jokers playing the fool on the way here."

Auntie Bee regards him through narrowed eyes for a minute, then decides to let it go. "Did you eat?"

Vincent snorts. "We're in the middle of a riot and you can still ask me if I ate?"

"Well? Did you?"

"Yes, Ma, I ate!" His head is turned away so I can't see it, but I can feel the eye roll even from the back seat.

"Good, good." She settles her black leather handbag on her lap and reaches up to smooth down a flyaway hair. "Good thing you came home from college today. Now let's go home and ask your baba what all this is about."

Vincent catches my eye in the rearview mirror, then quickly looks away. "Okay, Ma," he says quietly. "Okay."

As a child, I used to scrunch myself way down in my seat, so that all I could see was the sky, and pretend we were hurtling through the air. I do this now, sliding as low as I can to count every treetop that whizzes by in groups of three, tapping each one out on my knees and then with my feet, anything to keep from looking at the ground, which is littered with bodies—anything to keep from thinking about fire and knives, Saf and Mama, living and dying. Especially dying.

"Almost there," Auntie Bee says to me from the front seat, and I wriggle my way back upright to look out the window. The metal shutters of each storefront are pulled tightly shut, and the streets are deserted save for a group of Chinese men sitting calmly on wooden stools, engaged in what looks like typical Tuesday-evening coffee shop conversation, except for the thick iron pipes and sticks sharpened to menacing points laid casually across their laps and at their feet. "Aiya," Auntie Bee mutters under her breath when she sees them. "They're expecting trouble, I see."

"Who are they?" I ask.

"Let's just call them the neighborhood watch," Vincent says grimly, raising a hand in salute as he drives past.

The little white house sits slightly apart from those

around it, its gleaming stone surface a stark contrast to their weathered wooden flanks, marking those who dwelled within as atas: upper-class, affluent, well-off.

We slip off our shoes and enter through dark wood doors set with colorful stained glass, and Auntie Bee pauses to kiss her fingers and touch them lightly to a simple wooden cross that hangs beside the entrance, bowing her head in prayer and gratitude. I am both mesmerized by this little gesture of faith and jealous of her intimate relationship with God. It always bothers me that I can't seem to connect with Him the way people like Auntie Bee and Mama can. The way I used to.

My first memory of God is watching my parents pray together. I loved their sejadahs, the prayer mats Mama set out each time the call to prayer came drifting through the air. Mama's was a deep green, Abah's a soft blue gray, and each was woven in gold thread with pictures of a mosque, intricate flowers and vines intertwining all along the edges. I'd run my fingers along the pattern, playing with the fringe on the end of each, as they bent and straightened and bowed and kneeled toward Mecca. Abah would recite the verses aloud, his voice turning the unfamiliar words into a song, and I remember sitting close and letting the words wash over me and feeling . . . safe.

Mama taught me the letters of the Arabic alphabet

one by one—alif, baa, taa—and I used to sit with her each night after the evening prayer, concentrating hard as I tried to decipher the pretty swirls and curls in the pages of the Quran until I, too, could recite them all on my own.

The day I could recite the Al-Fatihah all by myself—the very first surah of the holy book, the surah that asks God to guide us to the straight path—I got my very first sejadah, its rich blue green set off with a golden-domed mosque.

Prayer meant asking God for his blessing and his forgiveness. Prayer meant thanking Him for everything he'd given us. And even I knew He'd given us so much.

But then Abah died. And I began to wonder what it was that I was supposed to be thankful for. And I haven't prayed since.

After the failed trip to the doctor, Mama read the Quran to me each night, determined to chase away the mischievous spirits wreaking havoc on my brain. No longer was she the scientific-minded nurse, once so skeptical of djinn and the supernatural; with no other options, my increasingly worrying symptoms had turned her firmly into a desperate, faithful believer. I didn't mind her doing it—I'd always found the verses beautiful, after all, and soothing—but I knew it wouldn't work. He had forsaken me.

God and I weren't currently on speaking terms.

"Don't say that, Melati," Mama would say. "God has a plan for all of us."

"Why is God's plan to make me this way?" I'd counter, and she'd purse her lips at my impertinence. But I went along with it anyway because it made her happy, and I'd do a lot worse to make my mother happy.

So we knocked on the door of every religious teacher and healer she could find, asking for their guidance, their wisdom to defeat the invisible enemy who held me so firmly in his grasp.

The first time, we had to take the bus out to Seremban, a two-hour journey on bumpy, winding roads. Our appointment was for two p.m.; we arrived nearly a half hour late, hot and tired, bones aching from the rattling of the bus. I was pale and queasy, having spent the ride fighting off both the Djinn and motion sickness; my mother was wound as tightly as a spring, tense from the stress of worrying about me and the bus and whether either of us would fall apart before we get there. "We're late," she said in clipped tones, clutching me by the arm, the better to both prop me up and hurry me along. "Come on, quickly, come on."

Our destination was one of a cluster of nondescript wooden houses on the outskirts of Seremban town. As my mother knocked hesitantly on the peeling blue door, a stray dog napping in the cool of the house's shadow peeled open one eye to glare balefully at us, and I found myself muttering, "Sorry," in its direction.

A young woman wearing a bored expression answered the door and ushered us wordlessly past a row of men and women waiting for their turn with the healer, into a dim, musty room lit only by two flickering oil lamps in the center of the room. The Djinn immediately reached up to clasp his cold hands around my throat, and I was suddenly, suffocatingly claustrophobic.

"Can't we crack open a window?" I asked Mama in a strangled voice.

"Shhhhh," she hissed back, staring expectantly at the door.

Soon enough, the healer swept in—Mama called him Ustaz, a title I'd only ever heard used for religious teachers and scholars before this. His floor-length robe was snow white and pristine, his straggly beard streaked with gray. "Sit, sit," he said, and we sat cross-legged on the woven straw mat across from him. "Now tell me your troubles," he said, and listened patiently as my mother poured out my whole story—the counting, the tapping, the pacing, the insomnia, the constant thoughts of her death—with the clinical precision of the nurse that she is.

Throughout it all, the ustaz nodded, regarding me over the top of his glasses, his gaze never wavering, while my cheeks burned and I looked down at the ground, trying to pretend none of this was about me. It all sounded so much worse when I was forced to listen to someone else list each one of my surreal maladies, each item to be handled and ticked off in turn.

"I see, I see," he said, once Mama was done. "Not to worry, madam; you've come to the right place." He turned to me. "Lie down, girl."

He made me lie flat on my back on the straw mat, my arms at my sides. Then he muttered verses from the Quran, all while swirling his arms and pulling vigorously at the air above me, his eyes closed in concentration. I knew it was meant to be a serious situation, but every time he flailed and grabbed at nothing and yanked at it, I felt perilously close to giggles. A snort escaped, and I quickly turned it into a cough-groan as my mother glared at me.

The ustaz stopped and opened his eyes. "There," he said, with great finality. "Now let me see here. . . ." He grabbed my toes and prodded each one hard, causing me to yelp in pain. "Yes, yes," he muttered, nodding. "You feel pain? That means the Djinn is there, definitely, definitely. Yes. I will help you with that."

He's not in my toes, I wanted to tell him. *He's in my chest, and stomach, and mostly in my head. My toes don't really have anything to do with it.* But I kept my mouth firmly shut. Adults rarely like being told that they don't have all the answers, or worse still, that the answers they do have are all the wrong ones.

He rummaged in the wooden chest beside him and emerged with three glass vials. "This one, you dab behind your ears and on your wrists, like perfume. One day, three times," he said, handing me the first one. "This one, you mix a little bit into your bathwater every time." I held the second vial to my nose and inhaled; it smelled like limes. "This one, I blessed with all the good Quran surahs already. You drink every day." The vials clinked against one another in my arms. "Okay," I said, then "Thank you." Should we shake hands? Was I supposed to bow? I didn't know what the etiquette was for a spiritual healing—I still don't.

He turned to my mother. "God willing, the Djinn will have completely left her body within the next three months."

"Three months? That long, ustaz?"

"You cannot rush God's work."

"Of course, of course," she said, subsiding hastily.

Before we left to catch the bus, I saw her slip a handful of notes into his outstretched palm. It was more money than we could really afford, and I felt the tips of my ears grow hot. Tears stung the back of my throat.

"Come on, Melati," she said, smiling at me. "Let's go home."

Truly, I did feel better that first time. I let the words of the holy book wash all over me, and came out feeling virtuous, cleansed, purified. I let myself believe that the Djinn was gone. This false sense of security meant I was unprepared for the onslaught when he returned later that night. *You thought it would be so easy?* The taunting lilt barely hid his anger. *You will see that you cannot be rid of me so easily.*

I couldn't stop counting that night. Couldn't stop tapping every third item in our house three times, and then again, and then again, caught in an exhausting loop I just couldn't break, my head filled with visions of Mama dying over and over and over again. I wailed and I raged and I sobbed, but I could not stop. And all she could do was stand there and watch, weeping quietly with me. "Take me to the madhouse, please," I told her at one point, weak and weary. "I can't live like this anymore."

"Never," she said, shaking her head firmly, the tears still visible on her cheeks. "And nobody ever will, unless they plan on killing me first."

She meant it too. She was determined to find something that would work. And so we went on, spending time and money on all sorts of treatments. I was subjected to cupping and needles, poked and prodded and induced to puke my guts out into a waiting basin, made to bathe with water laced with salt, with lime, with leaves and herbs and flowers. Each time, I willed myself to get better, to heal, to chase the Djinn out and leave me with my own thoughts at last. But now I had learned to distrust that beguiling, early feeling of peace.

And all the while, I watched as it took a toll on my mother. Mama used to be gay and vibrant; when she walked into a room, she drew your eyes to her like moths to a flame. My father's death a year before had diminished her light a little, but it was as if she'd gone from a wild, raging bonfire to a delicate, tapered candle—she was still bright and beautiful, but somehow more elegant in her grief. My situation took whatever light she had left and extinguished it. Before my very eyes, she shriveled and shrank until all that was left was shadows. The Djinn might inhabit my body, but he held us both captive.

By the fifth treatment, I finally figured it out. When Mama asked me how it went, guarded and cautious, I told her what she needed to hear. "I'm better now, Mama," I said. "I think it'll all be fine from now on."

"Really?" she asked me, her eyes filled with joyful tears, her voice high with grateful disbelief. "Really," I lied. And the Djinn smiled a vicious little smile and wrapped his scaly arms tight around my chest, as if he would never let go.

The day I gave my mother back her light, I vowed I would never let her know my darkness again.

• • •

"Who is this?"

We are barely five steps into the house when we are greeted thusly by another young man. Vincent might not have been too thrilled to see me earlier, but compared to the venom I can hear dripping from each word this one utters, we're practically best friends. My heart begins to pound, and my mind, sensing impending trouble, leaps immediately to the safety of the numbers and occupies itself counting the black-and-white tiles on the floor.

"Is this how you say hello to guests now, Frankie?" Auntie Bee regards him calmly, her hand hovering protectively on my shoulder. "This is Melati. She'll be staying with us until we can figure out how to get her home. Now, where's Baba?"

"Not home," Frankie says sullenly. "He hasn't come back yet. And we can't call him. All the phone lines are down."

My heart sinks at this; I was just about to ask if I could use the phone to call the hospital and speak to my mother. *She's not there anyway*, the Djinn insists, jabbing at my stomach with sharp spikes of fear. *She's dead. You didn't protect her. Just like you didn't protect Saf.*

My eyes fill with tears, and I concentrate even harder on the way the tiles fit together, counting off their perfect squares in threes.

"Okay, then—home soon, I'm sure," Auntie Bee says, making her way into the house and gesturing for me to follow. "Better make sure we have dinner ready by the time he gets here. He'll be hungry. Come, Melati," she says, turning to me. "I have some clothes you can change into."

I drift along behind her as she leads me down a long, narrow corridor. We pass three closed doors before she opens one on the right. It's a box of a room, just big enough to fit a narrow bed, a small vanity with an oval mirror and a white stool, and a chest of drawers. Auntie Bee rummages about in this for a while before emerging with a white blouse and a gray skirt. "My niece's clothes," she explains, handing them to me. "She studies at the university. Her parents are in Johor, so she stays here sometimes when she has a break. Aiya—" She breaks off suddenly, clicking her tongue. "I'd better find some way to contact her and make sure she's safe," she mutters. "The bathroom is there, across the hall. You change and come to the kitchen when you're ready, girl."

She disappears down the hall and I quickly slip into the bathroom. After I use the toilet, I wash my hands at the clean white sink and stare at myself in the mirror, taking in my disheveled hair, half out of its usual braid; the blue shadows under my eyes; the tracks of clean lines my tears have left in the layer of soot and dirt on my face. *The face of a betrayer*, the Djinn snarls, *a traitor, a deserter, a girl who runs away when the people she loves need her.*

I squeeze my eyes shut, gripping the sides of the sink for balance, tapping each with my fingers, three times on this side, then the other, then again, then again, then again. Then I strip off my filthy school uniform, folding the blouse and pinafore, which reek faintly of drain water, and placing them neatly on a little table by the door. I grab a blue washcloth hanging on a knob by the sink, and I scrub and scrub and scrub until my skin tingles and the stranger in the mirror disappears.

Back in the room, there are no underclothes, so I suppose the ones I'm wearing will have to do. Then I put on the other girl's clothes. The blouse is some type of linen, scratchy against my skin; I tuck it into the cotton skirt, which stops below my knees. I rebraid my hair, tidy myself up as best I can, and make my way out of the room, trying to ignore the fact that the Djinn hasn't stopped his steady stream of dark whispers and that my heart hasn't stopped its exaggerated beats since I got here. I don't even realize that I'm tapping to them as I walk, my fingers hidden in the depths of some strange girl's pockets.

In the kitchen, Auntie Bee has changed out of her elegant cheongsam into a high-necked cotton blouse in a soft blue gray and loose black pants. She whirls about, adding a pinch of salt here, tasting there, stirring this, chopping that. "Oh good, they fit!" she says when she sees me.

"Come, help me get this dinner on the table. Uncle will be hungry when he comes home." She says this calmly, but I have a lot of practice in hiding how I feel, and I can spot the telltale signs of worry any day: the white knuckles that grip the dishes tightly as she sets the table, the pauses between conversations that go just a hair longer than they should.

For lack of anything else to do, and desperate for something else to focus on so I can shut the Djinn up, I drift along in her wake, picking things up, putting them down again, tapping everything secretly three times, pretending that this can somehow be construed as helping.

There was a time when I loved being in a kitchen, when it was the center of our household, emanating delicious, mouthwatering smells and filled with laughter and conversation. Once upon a lifetime ago, I wasn't totally useless, either—I'm handy with a knife, which Abah taught me how to use properly years ago. "You hold it like this, Melati," he'd say, demonstrating. "You see? Curl your fingers against the blade like this, and then cut the onion like this." And there they were—perfect slices, every time.

These days, there's not that much laughter, and I'm not that much use. In my defense, it's hard to be much help to Mama when the Djinn keeps screaming ominous warnings and portents of doom: *That knife could slice a major artery and she would be dead before you know it.*

She could have a previously unknown, fatal allergy to one
of her ingredients for this curry she's made a million times.
She could choke, she could burn, she could scald. Mama's
kitchen is a cacophony of hazards, and I am too deafened
and defeated by them, too busy saving Mama's life with
my never-ending number chains to bother with such com-
monplace tasks as slicing onions.

"Lazybones," Mama would tease me as I sat watching her wash the rice for dinner, mesmerized by the sure,
graceful movement of her hands sifting through the grains
to remove the dirt and grit. I'd just laugh and let her believe
it, counting each grain as it slipped through her fingers.

Finally, Auntie Bee makes us sit down around the marble-
topped dining table laden with rice and dishes—chicken
stewed in an aromatic brown sauce, deep green leaves of
kailan sautéed with chili and garlic, steam rising gently
from the fragrant white rice in the bowl. "Eat, eat," she
tells us. "Everything is better with a full stomach. Don't
worry," she whispers to me, passing me a spoon in place of
the chopsticks I have no idea how to use. "Everything you
can eat, no pork in anything. Got chicken lah, but this is
darurat—emergency—surely God will forgive you."

"Thank you, Auntie," I whisper back. Obediently,
Vincent and I grab our bowls and begin to fill them; I
stay clear of the chicken, as if God cares anymore what I

do, and load up on vegetables. It seems strange to enjoy food at a time like this, but each bite of the crisp greens, the crunchy garlic, the heat of the red chilis, is such pure pleasure that I could cry.

As we eat, I keep my head bent and my eyes on my food; I can feel Frankie's eyes boring into my forehead from across the table. An explosion, I realize, is inevitable.

And so it is. "This is ridiculous, Ma," Frankie spits out, flinging his chopsticks down and crossing his arms tightly across his chest. "Why invite this Malay girl into our home? Why must we share our food with her when her kind don't even want to share a country with us?"

"Frankie." Auntie Bee clicks her tongue, her brow furrowed with irritation. "Show some respect."

"Respect? Respect?!" He snorts. "The killing started because her kind, those Malay cibais, started it." I want to ask what "cibai" means, but from the way he spits it out, I'm guessing it's nothing good. The Djinn thumps on my heart like a drum, grinning widely. "They think they can just whack us however they like and we'll roll over and take it, like good dogs." Frankie looks directly at me then, and I turn away, breathless with the force of his rage. I feel like I've been slapped. In my head, Frankie leads a band of armed thugs into Mama's hospital, shoots everyone in sight, then burns the entire building to the ground. Hidden beneath the table, my hands tap out my usual tattoo on my knees, but they're shaking so hard I keep losing track and having to begin again, over and over and over.

"Frankie." Auntie Bee's voice is soft, but there is a note of warning that hints at the steel lurking below.

If Frankie hears that note, he chooses to ignore it entirely. "But it's true, Ma. Our family has been here for generations! You always talk about our ancestors coming from China, leaving their homes to break their backs in the mines. And for what?" Frankie is practically spitting, so great is his anger. "The British got all the money for our work, and now the Malays want to do the same. The country was built on the labor of our people, and this is how they thank us for it? If they come poke at bees' nests, then too bad if they get stung."

"You sound like a child," Vincent says coldly. "They started it! They did it first!" he singsongs, sticking out his tongue in mock-playground fashion. I snort with laughter, then cough to hide it as Frankie shoots me a hostile look.

"You sound like a Malay suck-up, Vincent," he says coldly. "Who's a good little doggy, then?"

"Vincent. Frankie. Stop it," Auntie Bee snaps, her voice ringing with authority. The brothers subside, glowering at each other over the table, while I stare at my bowl of barely touched food, tapping my fingers lightly along the sides so nobody notices. "We have a guest in our house, and she will share our food and drink because I have invited her to do so. Surely I have taught you better than this."

"Sorry, Ma," Vincent says, shamefaced, while Frankie looks away, mumbling a halfhearted apology under his breath.

There is a sound then from the doorway. "Baba is home," Auntie Bee half sighs, her relief obvious, and it's only when I see her body relax that I realize just how tightly wound she's been waiting for his arrival.

She hurries to the door to greet him, ushering him to the table. "Come, Baba, eat, eat, you must be starving. Are you all right? Are you hurt?"

"Yes, yes, Bee, I'm fine," he says impatiently, waving her fluttering platitudes away like so many irritating flies. Uncle is a tall, thin man, his silver-gray hair and gold-rimmed glasses lending him a dignified air. He sits at the head of the table, nods to his two sons, and then finally takes in my presence.

"Hello," he says, looking at me over the rim of his spectacles. "Who is this?" The words, flung with so much hostility at me only an hour before, are spoken gently, curiously, this time around, and I find myself warming immediately to this kind-eyed man.

Auntie Bee reaches out to pat my hand. "This is Melati," she says. "She was at the Rex too. There was some . . . some trouble there. I had to bring her home with me."

He nods, as if it's entirely normal to bring home a random Malay child. "Of course, of course," he murmurs. "Sorry, I never introduced myself. You can call me Uncle Chong."

"Thank you for letting me stay, Uncle Chong," I say shyly.

"No, no," he demurs, stretching out his arms expansively. "Our home is your home." Frankie snorts imperceptibly into his rice bowl, and I catch Vincent throwing him a murderous look.

Auntie Bee fills his plate, and Uncle Chong talks. "I was having a drink with Osman after closing the shop," he tells us between bites. "We were near Osman's house, up by Jalan Gurney. Suddenly, we heard a huge roaring, a huge commotion, coming from Princess Road. Then we saw a young Malay fellow run past. Aiyo, the fear all over his face! I could feel it, even from where I was sitting. Then Ahmad from across the street yelled at us. 'They are rioting on Princess Road!' he said, 'Go home!' Osman and I said our good-byes—he bolted back to his house and I ran for the car and drove like a maniac. Didn't stop until I reached our gates."

He pauses to gulp down some water. "On my drive, I saw columns of smoke rising from different neighborhoods—Dato Keramat, Chow Kit. The city is burning, and who knows when it will stop?"

There is silence at the table. Vince is poking at his food with his chopsticks, deep in thought; Frankie is chewing furiously, his brows furrowed. Auntie Bee's eyes are closed, one hand over her mouth as though to keep her thoughts from spilling out. When she finally speaks, it's in a whisper.

"Why is this happening?" she says.

Uncle Chong sighs. "Hard to say, ah Bee," he replies. "You know lah, the government will say it's the Communists at work. Who knows? They could be right. But I think the truth is that this has been brewing for a long time, ever since we were working to gain our independence in fifty-seven. The Malays resent the Chinese for taking over the urban areas, getting rich while so many of them remain poor in the kampongs. . . ."

"As if that is our fault." Frankie sniffs. "Who asked them to be so lazy?"

Uncle Chong goes on as if he hasn't even spoken. "The government was divided even then. Some shouting about preserving ketuanan Melayu—Malay supremacy. Some trying to push for a Malaysian Malaysia, not just a Malay one. Some insisting the Chinese need to protect our own interests. And the Indians are left to gather whatever scraps they can. How do you expect unity to grow from seeds of self-interest? Look at those riots in Penang last year. . . ."

The Djinn's ears perk up at this, and he begins to pound gleefully on my heart, each *thud* echoing loudly in my ears. *The riots in Penang,* he says. *Don't those sound familiar?* I hate that he speaks. I hate that he reminds me. I don't need reminding. The hartal riots were how Abah died. *And now Mama will die the same way,* the Djinn crows. *Isn't that sweet?*

I can feel my cheeks burning. I zero in on my food bowl and begin to count all the grains of rice I can see, but only the perfectly white ones, untouched by even the merest hint of sauce or gravy. One, two, three, four, five, six, seven . . . Around me, the conversation continues.

"But why, though?" Vince says, his voice rising. "Why now? When did it get so bad? My friends and I, we're all different races, nobody says, *Oh, you're Chinese, we can't be friends,* or *Oh, you're Malay, guess you're on your own, then.* That's stupid."

"Some Malays—not all of you, my dear," he says reassuringly as he glances at me, "some Malays think the government has been giving the Chinese too much face."

"What does that mean?" Vince asks, frowning.

"It means they feel that they welcomed us into the country and in return we take from them—jobs, land, money—and the government doesn't do anything to stop it."

"But that's stupid," Frankie interjects. "This isn't Tanah Melayu anymore. This is Malaysia. When they declared independence from the British twelve years ago, it wasn't just the hard work of the Malays that did it, it was everyone—Malays, Chinese, Indians, everyone."

I'm too busy counting rice grains to focus properly on what he's saying, but somewhere in the dim recesses of my head where the Djinn doesn't lurk, I remember my history teacher Puan Aminah pointing out the obvious Hindu influences in the ruling kingdoms of ancient Kedah, the marriage of the sultan of Malacca to the Chinese princess Hang Li Po. "Do not ever let anyone tell you that you do not belong here," she had said, looking at us intently. "We all do. There is space for us all." Saf had leaned against me then—history always made her sleepy—and I remember so clearly the smell of her hair and the way it brushed against my face that I almost burst out in sobs right then and there.

Instead, I tap furiously against my knees, willing the tears away. I wonder if those men in the cinema, or the ones shouting Allahu akbar in the streets, were ever taught the same lessons.

Uncle Chong leans back in his seat, taking off his glasses and running his hand over his eyes. "You are right, son," he says slowly. "But when you are fighting for your rice bowl, you don't think about how many hands were needed to grow the grain. You only think about who's out to steal your portion. Do you see?"

The room is silent while everyone else contemplates Uncle Chong's words and I contemplate my own ever-moving fingers, intent on not losing count.

"I think I prefer the Communists," Auntie Bee says suddenly, and we all look at her. She shrugs. "What? Better an outside force we can unite against rather than the bickering that divides us from within."

We have barely finished the dinner we pretend to enjoy so as not to hurt Auntie Bee's feelings when it begins. From outside come the sounds of bangs, crashes, yells. Auntie Bee's face is pale. "Frankie, go and make sure the door is locked," Uncle Chong says, his face grim. "The gate, no need. Don't go outside. Vincent, you check the windows. Make sure everything is secure."

When they return, the five of us huddle around the large transistor radio in the living room, and through the crackle of incessant static we hear the words "emergency" and "twenty-four-hour curfew."

"What does that mean, Ba?" Vincent asks his father, who is pacing up and down the room, lost in thought.

"Hmm? It means we can't go out. We can't leave the house." Uncle Chong rubs his forehead, sighing.

"I . . . I can't go home?" I blurt out. My palms are damp with sweat; I wipe them off discreetly on my borrowed skirt, tapping as I go. I knew we were in the middle of something big, but for some reason I'd never equated that with not being able to go home. The idea of being away from Mama for so long makes me light-headed and clammy. The Djinn, sensing a weak spot, works out a particularly gory death scene. *Count, Melati*, he whispers, and I don't have the strength to fight him.

"We'll have to ration the food," Uncle Chong is saying. "Make sure nothing goes to waste."

Auntie Bee leaps to her feet. "I'll check what stocks we have in the pantry," she says, already making her way to the kitchen. Uncle Chong nods and walks out of the room. Approximately 608 counts of three later, he reappears, his arms laden with sticks, lengths of pipe, an assortment of tools. A heavy wrench slips from his grasp and falls to the ground with a loud *clang*.

"Just keep these close," he says, meeting our questioning gazes levelly. "Keep them close. You never know when you might need them."

He hands them out. Frankie claims a thick length of heavy iron pipe for himself, swinging it about to test its weight, and I wonder if he can hear the imaginary cracking of a thousand Malay skulls. Vincent takes a long stick and grasps it with both hands, his head bowed. Auntie Bee takes the wrench and prods me to choose a weapon; I grab a hammer and imagine what it would feel like to bash someone's brains out with it. Then I think about Saf, and how she was left—*How you left her*, the Djinn whispers—alone and defenseless, and I think I may throw up. *Count the floorboards; it will make you feel better*, he tells me, and I hate how readily I agree.

Uncle Chong sighs. "At least we're ready for anything," he says.

Then, from outside, we hear it. "Please! Please! Help us!" The desperate cries are punctuated with frantic pounding on the door, and we all immediately draw our weapons close. "Tolong, help, please! Open the door! Tolong!" The woman's cries are piercing and tinged with hysteria; in the next moment, a baby begins to bawl.

Before anyone can stop her—"Wait, Ma, it might be a trick!" Frankie hisses, to no avail—Auntie Bee strides across the room and flings the door open. A slight young woman with a hunted look in her dark eyes trips over the threshold in her eagerness to get inside and crumples on the floor. In her arms, the squirming bundle continues to bawl—a tiny little baby.

"Shhh, shhh." Auntie Bee strokes the young woman's back soothingly, but she can't speak and she won't let go of the child. For long minutes, the room is filled with the sound of her sobs and the child's wails, and all of us just stand and stare, uncertain of what to do next.

When she's finally calmed down, we learn that her name is Ann, and that she took the baby and ran for her life after their home was engulfed in smoke and fire.

"Nothing left," she says quietly, rocking the now-sleeping child in her arms. "All gone. Nothing left."

• • •

When we're all awake, it's easy to pretend we can't hear what's happening outside. But in the silence of the night, I lie awake, listening and absorbing every crash, every shout, and later, every gunshot.

The Djinn thrives in the chaos, wrapping his arms around me and whispering his poisonous thoughts in my ears gleefully. My mind races, cycling through scene after scene with every sound: Saf's lifeless body slumped in the seats of the Rex; Mama, doused in flames and screaming in agony; Frankie, a bloodied knife in his hands and a crazed grin on his face. I cower under the sheets on Vincent's bed, clutching my hammer and counting every single book on the shelves that line the opposite wall, then again by color, then alphabetically by title, then by author.

When that doesn't work, I slip out of bed and methodically begin to arrange them. In the back of my mind, deep in the recesses, where the Djinn can't seem to reach, I know this is irrational, stupid, crazy. I know just thinking about death won't cause my mother to die. I know that books on a shelf won't stop her from dying, no matter how I arrange them. But every time I try to stop myself, a cold, creeping dread envelops my entire body. *Are you sure? What if it's true? What if the moment you stop is the moment Mama dies? How can you be sure?* And I turn back to the safety of the numbers, fearful and shaken.

Eventually, I fall asleep on the floor in front of the

bookshelves, curled up with a copy of *The Old Man and the Sea* (H for Hemingway, first name Ernest, so it belongs on the fifth row, right between Hawthorne, Nathaniel, and Hesse, Hermann; I also take comfort in the fact that the title has six words, the first name has six letters, the last nine. The Djinn grins, baring his sharp teeth: three times lucky).

When I wake up, it's so early that the sun hasn't yet risen. My throat feels like sandpaper, and I'm desperate for a drink, so I open the door . . . and nearly trip over the body lying in front of it.

All over Auntie Bee's living room, packed from wall to wall and in every available inch of space, are people: men, women, children, Malay, Chinese, Indian. The chairs and tables are stacked in one corner of the room and piled high with a motley array of bags and baskets. Auntie Bee picks her way through the bits and bobs and bodies as best she can, holding a tray laden with goodies and handing out a drink here, a biscuit there, and a comforting pat or word to all. She sees me in the open doorway and makes her way over to me.

"Here you are, girl," she says, handing me a cup of steaming tea from the tray. "Drink, drink. It's good for you."

I take the cup and sip obediently. "Who are all these people, Auntie Bee?" I whisper.

There is a pause. "These are our neighbors," she says. "They had nowhere else to go. The people came with knives and gasoline and fire. Wooden houses, they burn so fast—it spread everywhere." I look at her in the dim early morning light and realize her face is wet with tears. "They burned them," she says, sighing. "They burned them, and now our friends have no homes."

I nod. I don't ask who "they" is. I'm not sure I want to know. Instead, I count the bodies in the room, three at a time, sipping my drink. The hot, hot tea burns my tongue and scalds my throat.

CHAPTER FIVE

"HERE YOU GO."

Vincent passes me a bowl filled with porridge so thin you can count the number of rice grains that went into it. With so many mouths to feed, and a twenty-four-hour curfew preventing us from making our way out for more supplies, Auntie Bee is trying her best to make do with what she has. As I force down mouthful after mouthful, the Djinn tickles my stomach with his sharp little claws and Mama withers away from hunger, trapped and alone. *Chew three times, swallow, chew three times, swallow. Chew three times, swallow.* After every third spoonful, I pause for a sip of water. Again and again, I sip, chew, swallow, until it's gone—the porridge, and the image of my mother's wasted body.

The rioting seems to have died down this morning, though when Frankie sticks his head out the window to see what's happening, there are immediate yells from the police officers patrolling the streets. "Get back inside now," a voice bellows, "or I'll blow your head off." Auntie Bee tugs at Frankie frantically—"Aiya, come inside now, come inside! Faster!"

Once he does, we quickly bolt the window. "The man was pointing a gun right at me," he says, his eyes wide with a mixture of fear and excitement. "Right at my head, here, see?" He points to a spot in the center of his forehead.

Auntie Bee shakes her head, her hand on her heart. "Don't ever do that again," she scolds. "Asking for trouble. If they don't blow your head off, I'll smack it so hard you'll wish they had."

Uncle Chong spends his time in front of reams of paper spread across the dining room table, the radio always on beside him, making lists, weighing options, sketching plans. The radio, which is kept on so we can hear the latest news, plays a constant stream of patriotic songs, as though admonishing us for not being better citizens. "We could go seek protection in another kampong," he muses. "Maybe here, or here." He jabs at a map laid out before him, scribbling on a notepad. "You two must be ready," he tells his sons, who stand close by, their eyes scanning the map eagerly. "We need to plan an escape route. If the mob comes, we must be ready to leave quickly and quietly." They make plans for a tunnel to be dug in the garden, behind the flowering jasmine shrubs, under the wall and out to the road and beyond. "That would work." Vincent nods, pushing back his chair to stand. "I'll go and get the shovels; I think Ma put them in the garden somewhere. . . ."

Frankie leans back in his chair. "I don't understand."

"What don't you understand?" Uncle Chong asks absently, busying himself with yet another list.

"Why don't we just ask the gang, the triad, to protect us?"

There is a pause as his father and brother both turn to stare at him. He shrugs. "What? They would."

"They're killing people," his father says slowly. "Killing our neighbors, our friends."

"They're killing Malays," Frankie corrects him. "They're killing the people who want to kill us. I don't see anything wrong with that."

Vincent rolls his eyes. "Right, it's perfectly fine that they're killing, so long as they're not killing us."

Frankie glares at him, a steely glint in his eye. "Ya. Why not? I'll do whatever it takes to protect our family. You think the Malays wouldn't do the same, if they get the chance?"

"None of the Malays I know would," his father says gently. "None of my friends would."

Frankie grunts and subsides. Vincent rolls his eyes and goes to look for shovels, and in my corner of the living room, I feel sudden, inexplicable tears prickling the back of my throat, threatening to spill out of my eyes and splash onto the tattered rug below.

I had a religious teacher in school one year who was very passionate about teaching us about the concept of hell. While others had spent their time taking us through the basic tenets of our religion, the nuts and bolts of worship, the grace and mercy of God, she seemed to enjoy dwelling on His more fire-and-brimstone qualities, lingering over the agonies that awaited us come Judgment Day. "And this is why you must heed the lessons of the Quran," she would intone solemnly, her eyes alight with a righteous fervor.

Nothing she told us in that class prepares me for the hell I live through in those first few days at Auntie Bee's house.

We spend our days packed with the neighbors into the gleaming white house on the hill, too afraid of the men with the hard eyes and the easy way with guns to risk leaving. Uncle Chong plays at optimism, telling us every day that "you see, things are getting better, any day now sure everyone can go home, don't worry." The houseguests are a motley assortment of stragglers: Ann and her baby, fair little Peggy with the shock of wispy dark hair, who seems to sleep most of the time and wail the rest of it; a white-haired, sari-clad Indian lady who calls herself Paati and who doesn't say much, but makes her way into the kitchen each morning and insists on helping Auntie Bee prepare meals; Fairos, who strokes his thin mustache and radiates unease every time Frankie is in the same room, and often tries to talk to me "Malay to Malay," which makes me uncomfortable; Auntie Letty and Uncle Francis, a Chinese couple who seem to be great friends with Auntie Bee and Uncle Chong; their twelve-year-old daughter, Annette, and her great friend Simone, who had been ready to spend the night at their house when everything fell apart.

The sight of them, arm in arm, whispering confidences to each other in quiet corners, so firmly entangled that it is hard to know where one ends and the other begins, reminds me painfully of Saf. And the Djinn, as always, knows just where to jab at me so that his words leave the deepest wounds. *That's what you and Saf used to be*, he taunts me. *Always together, except when it mattered most. And now Mama is next.* Every hour brings a fresh glimpse of death: Saf's, my mother's, both, together, individually, my fault every time. *You failed them. You failed them. You failed them.* I sacrifice every minute to the altar of the Djinn, tapping on this, counting that, over and over and over again, yet never getting to that moment when things felt "just right," when my brain might stay quiet, when I can take in air and feel like I am actually breathing. Once or twice, I think I see Auntie Bee staring at me, her expression worried, but she leaves me alone.

When there is so much broken about the world we currently live in, one cracked person is easy enough to excuse or ignore.

On the third day, acrid, pungent gas steals in through the cracks in the doors and windows, and I wake up in Vincent's bed coughing and gasping for air, tears streaming down my cheeks. At first, I think this is the end. The Djinn has finally decided to destroy me. Every breath burns a path straight through my body, and I feel as if my lungs are filled with fire.

This is death, I think to myself, rubbing desperately at my stinging skin, my swollen eyes. *This is how you die.* I curl up in my borrowed bed and will the end to come quickly. If I'm honest, some small part of me thinks it might almost be a relief.

Instead, Auntie Bee bustles into the room with a pail full of cold water and a cloth to gently wipe away the worst of the pain. "Tear gas," she murmurs from behind the damp rag she's tied over her own mouth and nose. I just nod. I'm not even sure what that is; all I know is that it hurts to breathe.

The authoritative voice that comes crackling over the radio informs us that the curfew will be lifted for two hours, and we all breathe a collective sigh of relief. "We can finally go home," Auntie Letty says, wiping away her tears. "Not home, Letty," Uncle Francis says, handing her in case." They set off, armed with heavy wooden sticks, and I see Auntie Bee pause by the door to stroke the little wooden cross, her head bowed. My heart is heavy with worry, and I can't sit still; in my head, the Djinn adds them to the lineup as the latest stars of my own personal horror movies, their lives seeping away each time I shut my eyelids. *Stop*, I tell myself, *stop thinking it, stop, you don't want this, stop*. But I can't.

I move around the room, touching each book and ornament, three quick, light little taps each time.

"Would you stop fidgeting and sit down? You're making me nervous," Auntie Bee implores me. So I sit and tap my feet instead, three times a side, willing the time to pass quickly and for Uncle and Frankie—yes, even Frankie—to make it home in one piece.

We sit this way in silence for a while. Then, suddenly, Auntie Bee speaks. "We used to live in Kampung Baru, you know, girl? Years ago, when the boys were both this small," she says, bringing her hands down to indicate a level just below her waist. "Uncle had a shop there. That's where you live, right?"

I nod. "Why did you leave, Auntie?"

"Oh, you know. The Malays didn't like us very much." She pauses and thinks about this for a second. "No, that's not true. They liked us fine, I think. They accepted us. We were part of their scenery. We had plenty of customers; the

his handkerchief. "Not home. But maybe we can ma[ke]
to your sister's house in Cheras. It'll be safer there."

One by one, they all make plans to head home or [to]
relatives with whom they can shelter for the rest of [the]
duration. I know Auntie Bee is sad to see them go. I kn[ow]
better than anyone what it feels like to want to prot[ect]
the people you care about. But she merely bustles aroun[d]
packing food, making sure everyone gets a bite to ea[t,]
arranging for the old Indian lady—"Paati," she insists, jal[b-]
bing at her chest, "You call Paati"—to get a ride to wher[e]
ever she needs to go.

I can tell Uncle Chong is relieved too at this lifting o[f]
the curfew; there have been enough mouths to feed that
we've all been feeling the pinch of subsisting on watery,
unsalted porridge, unripe bananas plucked prematurely
from Auntie Bee's trees, and boiled sweet potatoes and
sweet potato leaves. We're in desperate need of provisions
to keep us going through however many more days we'll
be here.

Watching the others leave, I ache to get out, find my
mother, keep her safe. Hidden in my pocket, my fingers
tap an ode to my desires. "Not yet," Uncle tells me gently.
"Not until we know more. Young ladies shouldn't be out
and about right now. Wait first, girl."

When the announcement is made, Uncle Chong takes
Frankie with him and tells Vincent to stay behind, "just

boys had plenty of friends to play with. I think it was the idea of us that they didn't like. You know lah, they would never say it straight out—Malays are so particular about giving face. But once in a while, someone would joke about pendatang, immigrants. Or they would refer to us as 'you Chinese,' laughing as they did it. Or make pointed little remarks about 'outsiders' stealing jobs." She sniffs.

The phrases are familiar; I feel a distinct, unsettling sting when I realize that I grew up with them, heard them so often they were reduced to nothing more than background noise. *Taking away our opportunities. Heathens. Chinese pigs. Go back to where you came from. Malaysia for the Malays.* Have I ever said any of those words? Do I believe any of it? The Djinn moves suddenly, rising from the depths, seizing this new idea gleefully. *Maybe you haven't. Maybe you will. Or maybe you already have. Haven't you?* Have I? I shake my head a little, trying to dislodge that needling voice, then shoot Auntie Bee a quick glance to see if she noticed. But she's still wrapped up in her memories.

"We didn't really mind too much lah, not at first," she continues, a faraway look on her face. "Or at least we tried not to. You Malays have this saying: Di mana bumi dipijak, di situ langit dijunjung. Do you know it?"

"No, Auntie."

"It means where you plant your feet is where you hold

up the sky." She smiles slightly at my confused face. "Wher ever you are, you must follow what the people there do, their customs, their ways," she explains. "So we did. We bit our tongues when people whispered things behind our backs, or made those sharp little comments to our faces, or even spit on our door. We paid Alang our fees regularly, so hooligans wouldn't cause us trouble. You know Alang?"

I nod. Everyone knows Alang. He and his gang rule Kampung Baru, demanding protection money from residents and shopkeepers to keep their properties safe from harm, walking through the neighborhood with a swagger in their step, daring anyone to cross them. Nobody ever does; Alang has a short temper, a long list of grudges, and a very sharp knife.

She sighs. "Everyone did it. We knew he asked us for more than our neighbors. But we paid anyway. No choice. What to do? That was our sky."

Auntie Bee leans back, rubbing her forehead. "Vincent was always a happy child. We never had to worry about him. And he was so young. He didn't really notice these things. But Frankie was so sensitive. He took all those little sharp pokes and kept them in his heart. He started talking back. He started getting into fights. He let them make him bitter." She sighs. "We left as soon as we realized what it was doing to him to stay. Luckily, your uncle is a hard worker; he got the shop he has now and made it pay. But we were too late. Those Kampung Baru fools gave Frankie a chip on his shoulder that's weighed him down ever since."

By the time they return, panting, arms laden with provisions, the sky is deepening to a mellow purple, streaked with orange from the rays of the setting sun, and in my head they have died thirteen times. Auntie Bee hovers around them anxiously. "Are you all right?" she asks, eyes scanning their bodies for signs of injury. "Are you hurt? Faster, tell me!"

"We're fine, Ma," Frankie says irritably, untangling himself from her arms. "Here, we got some stuff for you." He deposits the bags by the door and heads off for his room.

"Not much, ah Bee," Uncle Chong says quickly. "There isn't much. The shops were smashed, you see. People have gone already, taken a bunch of things, looting. We could only get a few more things. Potatoes, one small bag of rice, some others . . ."

Auntie Bee is busy perusing the bags, clicking her tongue in frustration. "Aiya," she mumbles to herself. "Oh, well. We make do."

She glances at her husband. "How was it?" she asks quietly.

He looks away, occupies himself rubbing at a spot of dirt on his trousers. "The streets are empty. Barricades everywhere, some with police, some with . . . others. A lot of burned-down buildings. Some . . . some bodies."

He gulps. "I saw one woman . . . They'd slashed her belly. There was a tin of milk powder nearby; it must have rolled out of her hands. She was brave enough to go get milk for her child, and that's what she got for it." He takes off his glasses, rubbing his eyes. "I hope wherever that child is, that he got some milk. I hope he's safe."

He looks up then and notices me standing nearby, shivering despite the evening heat. "I'm sorry, Melati," he tells me, shaking his head. "I don't think you'll be able to go home any time soon."

That night, counting the books from my usual spot in Vincent's bed, I hear a sudden shriek and race outside, my heart pounding, gripping my hammer.

Auntie Bee is on her knees in the middle of the floor, her face ashen, weeping. Uncle Chong kneels beside her, his arms around her shoulders, trying his best to console her. Vincent leans against a nearby wall, arms crossed, his face grim. "What's happening?" I ask him, doing my best to conceal my fear.

"Frankie's gone." He sighs. "His bed is empty. He must have snuck out in the night while we slept." He looks at his parents and shakes his head. "How can he do this to them? He may be my brother, but that stupid son of a bitch better be careful, because if those goons out there don't kill him, I just might."

In the early hours of the morning, after a night where none of us slept and Auntie Bee merely sat on the settee, rocking back and forth and refusing to eat, drink, or speak, Frankie slips into the house.

Under each arm, he holds two transistor radios. Two chickens, feet tied together with a length of rope, hang limply over one shoulder. "Hello!" he greets us cheerily, slipping his shoes off at the door. Vincent and I look at each other, then at Auntie Bee, who straightens and stands to look at her son.

"Where have you been?" she asks clearly, the first time we've heard her voice in hours.

"I remembered that one of those houses in the back road, they keep chickens," he says, gesturing at the birds on his shoulder. "There's a rooster that's always waking me up in the morning. I thought, *Chicken, good, we can have something more to eat.* So I slipped out and went to catch some. I was so fast, so quiet, nobody even heard me. I walked right behind some soldiers and they never even turned!" He smiles, delighted with himself. "When I got there, the buggers were roosting, so they didn't hear me coming. I just grabbed one and held it hard by its neck until it snapped. Then I did another one." I gulp back a painful lump in my throat, imagining Frankie's powerful hands wringing the life out of a chicken who never even realized what was coming. I eat chicken all the time—Mama makes a chicken-and-potato curry so delicious that it makes my mouth water just to think of it—and I know that even chickens killed the halal way would probably have preferred not to be killed at all. What gets me is the expression on Frankie's face, the light in his eyes as he describes killing another living thing so easily. He looks so . . . proud of himself.

Look how happy that Chinese pig is, the Djinn whispers. *If that's how he treats innocent animals, how do you think he'd treat people he actually hated?*

Shut up, I tell him, *shut up, shut up*. I say it three times to be safe, and hate myself for doing it.

"And the radios?" Uncle Chong asks. I can hear the whisper of steel in his words, but Frankie, oblivious, rattles on. "Well, the houses were all empty; their windows were all smashed in and everything. So I went in and saw all this stuff, and I grabbed these two radios. Now Vince and I can have one each!" He grins, victorious, as happy as a child.

Before we can react, Auntie Bee is striding across the room. The harsh *crack* her hand makes as it comes into contact with Frankie's cheek echoes through the room; her palm leaves a red mark on his pale skin. He steps back, his face stunned.

"You make me ashamed to call you my son," his

mother says quietly. Then she turns and walks slowly back to her room, shutting the door behind her with a firm *click*.

When we wake up the next day, there is fried chicken on the table, its skin crispy and golden brown, its flesh juicy and tantalizing. I can't eat it, can't look at it without thinking of Frankie's hands wrapped around its neck. But Uncle Chong and Vince and the neighbors we call to come over, they eat and eat and eat until there is nothing left but a pile of bones, savoring every mouthful.

Auntie Bee doesn't take a single bite.

CHAPTER SIX

THE DAY WANES ON, AND we all do our best to take our minds off the fighting all around us. Uncle Chong, Frankie, and Vince work on digging the tunnel below the wall in the back garden, behind the flowering shrubs of jasmine. The steady *clink, clink, clink* of their shovels against the dirt is soothing, and in my head I count along: *one, two, three, one two three, one, two, three*, just like music. Unbidden, the words of a Beatles song float through my head as they so often do, this time a strange little song about a girl with kaleidoscope eyes. It's not my favorite; John sings lead on this and not Paul, so to me it's automatically not as great as it could be. But there's something about the lyrics, so lavish and so odd—tangerine trees, marmalade skies, rocking horse people, marshmallow pies—that send colors shooting through my head, like fireworks.

As they immerse themselves in their task, often pausing to consider their progress and discuss their options—"You think we need it bigger?" "No lah Ba, we should keep it this size, so it isn't easy to find." "But what if some of the fatter villagers cannot fit? You know how big Uncle Maniam has gotten since he got married!"—I sing softly under my breath and prod through the upturned earth, looking for five fairly smooth stones of roughly the same size. The music, the beat, the act of methodically rooting through the dirt—all of this helps to keep the Djinn mercifully silent, or at least to drown out the worst of his whispers.

In the afternoon, when the heat forces the men back indoors, we sit on the back porch and I do my best to use the stones to teach Vince the intricate throwing and catching motions that make up the game of Batu Seremban, which my girlfriends and I played incessantly as children; in return, he shuffles through a worn deck of playing cards and tries to teach me the rules of gin rummy. We are both terrible.

"This would be so much better if we could bet on it," he mutters, clenching his jaw and narrowing his eyes in concentration as he flings one stone straight up in the air and quickly attempts to sweep up the four on the ground in time to catch it. Only he messes up and ends up scattering the stones every which way, sending them clattering loudly against the wooden floorboards. He clicks his tongue in frustration. "You see? I have no incentive to get it right."

"Why must you Chinamen gamble on everything?" I tease him.

"Why are you Malays so backward that you have to play with rocks?" he retorts back.

We spend the evening in his room. He leaves the door open for propriety's sake, yet my body still buzzes with a nervous energy that won't let me stay still. Is it the Djinn? Is it something else? I don't know. Instead, I drift from here to there, touching this, picking up that, running my fingers along the belongings I'm starting to know as well as my own. The tin of musky pomade and the orange plastic comb that lie on the shelf beneath the speckled mirror on the wall. The family picture in a simple gold frame by his bed: Auntie Bee staring straight at the camera, hair perfectly coiffed for the occasion, Uncle Chong with glasses far too big for his face, smiling his warm smile, a small Frankie looking sullenly at the photographer in a starched sailor suit, and a tiny Vince, a smile splitting his face in two, a tendril of drool shining on his chin, snug on Auntie Bee's lap. The notebooks lining the worn wooden desk like sentinels, each filled from cover to cover with surprisingly neat handwriting, small and straight, each stroke thick and assured. And all along one wall, bookshelves filled with the books I've come to know so well. There are 115 altogether, or there were—it wasn't divisible by three, a fact that caused me so much anxiety and grief that eventually the Djinn demanded I slip one book out of the case and put it on the shelf in the living room instead. I glance at him as he runs his hands over the remaining 114 and wonder if he notices their missing comrade, but he's more preoccupied with the fact that I've rearranged them.

"Did you alphabetize them?" His voice has a note of amused disbelief that makes me flush bright red.

"I just . . . like things to be organized," I say. The Djinn sends notes of panic creeping delicately up my spine. *Look at him*, he whispers. *He knows what you are. He knows you're strange and broken. And if he knows that, he'll know eventually that Saf dying and Mama dying—those are both your fault.* I clench my teeth and tap every third book on the shelf lightly, three times each. I try to make it look as if I'm just browsing, but I think I see Vince's eyes on my fluttering fingers. I think I see him frown slightly. I think, but I'm not sure, because I can't look right at him, can't stop until the Djinn is satisfied and the world feels right again.

If Vince does notice, he says nothing. He just strokes the spine of each book lovingly, like old friends or lovers, and sighs. "Ba says I think too much of books," he says, and something in his voice, so quiet, so gentle, soothes the itch in my brain so that I can calm down and actually focus on what he's saying. "I'm studying English, you know, at college? They . . ." He jerks his head in the general direction of the living room, where we can hear the low buzz of the radio, which is never switched off these days. "They wanted me to study business, go into an office, be a big shot. But I hate numbers." He smiles and shrugs. "I'm a major disappointment."

Vince pulls out his prized record player then, and my heart soars at the sight of the shiny deep red box, the idea of listening to music again, the only time the Djinn seems to stay away. I sink down on the floor beside him, the voice and my nerves both gone for now, eager to hear my old friends. I'm not sure I realized until then just how much I'd missed them.

When the first notes come, it's as if my brain is being enveloped in a comforting hug. For the first time in days, I can feel my body unclench, the tension receding. For the first time in days, I feel like me.

He puts on record after record, keeping the volume on low so as not to attract too much attention, selecting them one after another from an enviable collection that he keeps in boxes under his bed. His choices surprise me: First, an intricate, delicate piano nocturne; then a swinging rock 'n' roll number; then a keening Chinese melody made no less sad by my inability to understand the words; then the familiar swell and lilt of an old P. Ramlee song.

I lean back against his bed and let the familiar words wash over me. Saf and I watched this movie together just a few years ago; P. Ramlee movies were the only ones her father grudgingly approved of, on the grounds that "Malays must support other Malays." I remember hearing this song for the first time, P. Ramlee's voice swirling around us in the dark theater, deep and soft and warm as an embrace. He sings of love and loss, every word laden with quiet despair. *Where will I find another*, he asks, *another quite like you?*

I think of Saf, and my heart crumples. From deep in my belly, I feel the Djinn start to stir, the shadows starting to creep in. *Stop*, I think. *Stop.*

"Can you play something else?" I know Vince hears that unmistakable crack in my voice, the one all my grief threatens to come rushing through. But he doesn't mention it.

"What would you like?" he asks instead.

"Play a Beatles song. Any Beatles song."

The rain beats a steady rhythm on the roof, and Paul McCartney's familiar voice fills the room, imploring us to try and see things his way.

Abah loved the Beatles, and this song was one of his favorites. Whenever he was in trouble with Mama—for turning up in clothes caked in mud and blood from a particularly thrilling mission; for stuffing me with too many pieces of bread slathered in sticky, sweet coconut jam that was meant to be an occasional treat; for buying me yet another record, "as if we were made of money," she sniffed—he'd grab her by the waist and swing her around. "We can work it out," he'd croon in her ear. She'd forgive him every time.

This song in particular, he used to tell me, was perfect for them. "You hear it? Listen closely now." He'd put the record on and I'd frown, concentrating furiously on the notes that wafted through the air. "You see? This is McCartney, all optimism and light—we can work it out, we can do this, all set to this upbeat pop tune. That's me, foolishly hopeful." He laughed, and I laughed too. It was true; Mama used to say that Abah was far too idealistic to be a police officer, that he never wanted to believe that people were capable of doing bad things. "Then the bridge . . ." The tempo changes to a lilting 3/4 time. "You hear that? Life is very short; there is no time—this is all Lennon, impatient, needing things to be done at once, no time to waste. That's your mother! Efficient to a fault. And it even sounds like those waltzes she loves."

He sighed and sat back, and I mimicked him, sitting in silence as the song washed over us. "Total opposites in so many ways. But when they get it right, don't they make the most gorgeous music together?" I wanted to ask him if he meant Lennon and McCartney, or him and Mama. I never did.

Before I realize it, my cheeks are wet with tears, and Vincent is looking at me in panic. "What, what is it, what's wrong?" he asks, running his hand through his hair, distressed at my sudden sadness.

"It's nothing," I tell him, trying to smile. "I . . . I miss my mother. It's just the two of us, you know? So it's strange that right now I'm just . . . one of me."

He nods, and I can tell that he understands, that he is trying to find the words to console me. "I'm sure she's all right," he says gently. "She's a nurse, you said? She must be very smart. She knows how to take care of herself. She'll keep herself safe, you'll see."

We fall silent again, and I tap to the beat, counting it out under my breath, trying to will away the anxious buzzing in my chest.

"Mel, what happened to your father?" Vince says it softly, and I know he's trying to be gentle, trying not to poke at old wounds too much.

I wipe away the tears and look down at my feet, counting it out, trying to keep my breathing steady, even. The Djinn is needling me again: *You can't trust him, you can't trust him, he'll think you're crazy, he'll leave you.* Across the room, Vince sits in silence, waiting it out with me. With my mind as unquiet as it is, I've come to appreciate Vincent's ability to stay still, to be patient, to let the thoughts come. *How much should I tell him?* I ask myself. *How far do I go?*

I glance at him. He's sitting on the floor, cross-legged

by the player surrounded by record sleeves, chin propped on his hands, arms propped on his knees, looking right at me.

I take a deep breath.

"My father was a police officer," I begin, and he draws his knees up toward his chest, clasping them with his arms, his attention fully focused on me. "It's just me and my mother now, but it wasn't always, not until just over a year ago. He was a kind man, generous, responsible. He loved music—especially the Beatles, and he taught me to love them too. And he was funny—he was SO funny. Nobody could make us laugh like he could. My mother loved him, and he worshipped her; you could see it in the way they looked at each other. I was their only child, and I know that made them sad sometimes—they wanted more, but it never happened. Still. We were happy."

I pause, trying to gather my thoughts. Vince doesn't move; as far as I can tell, he barely breathes.

"Then in late November that year, in 1967, he got the call. They told him he had to go to Penang. Some trouble up there, Malay and Chinese nonsense, he told us. They were sending extra personnel from KL to help smooth things down. My mother didn't want him to go. She didn't say so, but I could tell from the way she bit her lips while she ironed his uniform, the way she clenched her fists when they talked about it. She worried all the time whenever he had these assignments, and so did I. But he told us he'd be back before we knew it. He kissed my mother, and then he kissed me, and he told me . . . he told me . . ."

"What?" Vincent asks me. "What did he tell you?"

"Life is very short," Paul and John sing in perfect harmony, "and there's no time for fussing and fighting." I swallow a sudden lump in my throat. "He told me, 'Take good care of your mother while I'm gone.'"

But you haven't done that, have you, Mel? You've ruined it, the Djinn's voice hisses. An image of Mama surfaces, lying facedown on a deserted road, blood trickling from her limp body and trailing lazily into an open drain nearby.

I sigh, rubbing my aching head. "He was dead the next day. There was a scuffle between some gang members. Somebody split his head open with a parang. Mama played this song for days afterward, weeping every time." I take another deep breath, letting the air fill my lungs, counting three beats, before I exhale and continue. "So you see, that was what I was supposed to do. Take care of her, keep her safe. And I'm not doing that, am I? I haven't seen her or spoken to her in almost a week, I have no idea where she is, what she's doing, if she's hurt. I'm failing my parents in so many ways." I can hear my voice rise, ragged with frustration, and I pause, fighting to stay in control.

The room is silent, the song having long reached its

conclusion. I feel the world shift, and I'm dizzy with the sense of release—this isn't a story I've ever told anyone, except for Saf. For one fleeting moment, I wonder if I should continue—if I should tell him how, ever since we got the call, ever since we buried my father, I dream endlessly of my mother's death. I wonder how he would react if I told him about the panic, the anxiety, the choking fear that my thoughts are ominous portents of my mother's future. I wonder if I should tell him about the Djinn.

I wonder what he'd think of me then, if he knew all of this.

Then the moment passes. I don't have to wonder. I know. He'd think what anyone would think, what our whole extended family thought when Mama and I came asking for help, when I was so exhausted, so full of images of death and numbers that I thought I was going insane. They told her I was crazy, possessed; that we had made God angry with our faithless lifestyle; that I needed a doctor or a bomoh or a cell at an asylum for the insane. It didn't happen overnight; the abandonment was so gradual that I didn't even know it was happening until one day I realized that it had been six months since we last saw my aunts or uncles, or any of the half-dozen cousins that used to come over to listen to records and braid my hair. I was a curse, they told my mother, and they wanted nothing to do with me.

And Vince will think the same.

So I bite my tongue and let the silence stretch on unbroken. Vince stares at his feet, lost in thought.

Suddenly, he rouses himself and speaks. "You know jasmine?" he asks. It's such a jarring change of subject that all I can do is look at him.

"Huh?" I say. "Like the flower?"

"Jasmine," he repeats, looking at me. "That's what your name means, right? Melati? Mama grows it, out in the garden. They're the bushes right in front of our escape tunnel." I nod, but I'm still confused, and it's written all over my face.

"Jasmine flowers are so pale, so delicate," he says, "you'd think they couldn't survive in this relentless tropical heat. But they thrive on it. They grow strong and gorgeous, and they bloom. Their perfume is . . . intoxicating, so strong that it leaves its mark on you long after you've left it behind."

He smiles. "I think that's pretty special, don't you?"

I smile back, and I don't feel a single urge to count anything at all.

CHAPTER SEVEN

ON THE FIFTH DAY, HAVING slipped out to procure more supplies, Vincent comes home bearing a bag of rice and an official-looking piece of paper, which he hands to Auntie Bee silently as we sit peeling potatoes in the kitchen and I try not to imagine my mother being sliced up by a vicious mob.

"What is this?" Auntie Bee asks, holding the paper in one damp hand and a potato in another and squinting vaguely at it.

"It's a curfew pass, Ma," Vince says. His voice is quiet, but I can tell from how he's standing, his body stiff and tense, that he's anticipating a fight.

"A curfew pass? Where did you get this?"

"I went and signed up with the Red Cross today, Ma. They need volunteers—I heard it on the radio."

Auntie Bee hands the paper to me and I skim the words quickly as she turns her attention back to the potatoes. "And what did you go and do that for?" she says nonchalantly. Her voice is calm, steady, but I can see her hands tremble ever so slightly as she lightly shaves off strips of brown potato skin, revealing the creamy flesh beneath.

Vincent half smiles; he isn't fooled. "There are a lot of people out there who need help," he tells her. "A lot of people trapped where they are, without any food to get through the days. A lot of people who might be hurt, who need medicine, doctors, hospitals—"

"Aiya, you." A ghost of a smile plays on his mother's lips. "I remember when you were little," she says. "Whenever some child was being bullied, whenever everyone decided they didn't want to play with one particular girl or boy, whenever someone fell down in the playground, there you were. Always wanting to save everyone, even then."

"Someone has to, Ma." His tone is gentle but firm. "If we stay inside and do nothing, then what's the use?"

"And if you get hurt?" Auntie Bee says as I hand the pass back to him. My heart begins to pound as I see knives pierce Vince's fair skin, the life drain from his eyes as fast as the blood from his veins. *He's going to die*, the Djinn whispers. I grip my paring knife so hard my knuckles turn white, and I count the potatoes in the basin in front of me. *Three, six, nine, twelve.* I tap my tongue against the roof of my mouth with each beat. Again, I feel like Vince is watching me, and my heart skips crazily at the idea of being seen. But when I look at him, his face is impassive, and he's focused entirely on his mother.

"Then I get hurt." He shrugs. There's no bravado, no beating of his chest; he says it as matter-of-factly as if he were talking about the weather.

"When do you start?" I ask him.

"As soon as I can." He walks out of the room, folding the precious piece of paper carefully as he goes. Auntie Bee leans back on her kitchen stool, closes her eyes and lets out a long sigh. The resigned sadness on her face makes my heart break a little.

"Are you all right, Auntie?" I ask gently.

Her eyes fly open. "Fine, fine," she murmurs immediately, rearranging her face back into its usual amiable expression, busying herself with potatoes. "Just tired, girl. After this, you go take some pucuk ubi for me outside? That will make a nice change, hmm?"

"Okay, Auntie," I say, busying myself with the business of plucking tapioca leaves from the garden and pretending I didn't see the way Auntie Bee's eyes glistened with unshed tears.

Later, as we listen to records, Vince shows them to me—the sticker for his car, the band he's meant to wear around his arm. "The pass lets me drive around during curfew," he explains, "but at least when people see me coming they'll know I'm a Red Cross volunteer. They'll know I'm there to help."

I nod, running my fingers over the bright red insignia sewn onto the band, tapping it quickly three times on each corner for luck. Frankie saunters in. He's not spent much time with any of us since his mother slapped him—"Aiya, he likes to sulk, been that way ever since he was a small boy," she sniffs.

"What's all this, little brother?" he says, picking up the band for a closer look.

"I'm a Red Cross volunteer now," Vince says.

The older boy snorts. "You've always been a bleeding heart," he says, shaking his head and tossing the strip of cloth contemptuously on the bed.

"What do you suggest we do with our hearts instead?" Vince's voice is even, but his eyes glint dangerously. I concentrate on making myself as small as possible, concentrate on not being seen. I don't want to be drawn into this fight.

"Forget hearts, we should be out there, with them!" Frankie gestures to the window. "You know all the gangs are outside there now, defending us, defending their territory? We should be defending our own! We should be giving hell to all the Malays who think we don't belong here and want to chase us out!" He pauses to shoot me a look. I clench my fists and force myself to meet his gaze without blinking.

"At very least," he says, when he finally turns back to Vince, "at very least, you should be sending your supplies only to people like us. Only to the Chinese. You should be helping your people."

Vincent sighs. "Frankie . . . your people, my people, our people, they're everyone. They're Malaysians. It's not Malays killing Chinese or Chinese killing Malays. It's stupid people killing stupid people."

He sits down on the edge of the bed and picks up the band, smoothing it against his knee. "I can do more for our people by taking up supplies instead of sticks," he says quietly. "I'd rather help with the healing than the hurting."

Frankie shakes his head. "Then you're too far gone to realize that your helping is what's hurting us." He turns on his heels and stalks out of the room.

Vince puts another record on—another Beatles number, as if he knows this is just what I need. I shoot him a grateful look, but say nothing. No words are necessary.

Music swells to fill the growing silence.

In the darkest hours of the night, when there's a particular quality of stillness to the world that makes it feel like you're the only one that exists, the Djinn rises. *Keep your end of the bargain*, he whispers softly in my ear. *Or do you think you'll enjoy the feeling of their blood on your hands?*

I sit up and listen for any movement in the house. Sat-

isfied that I'm the only one awake, I slip out of bed, clear a
space in the middle of the room, and begin.

Six steps, pivot. Six steps, pivot. Six steps, pivot. My
feet trace three straight lines, a perfect triangle. *Perfect?*
Are you kidding me? The Djinn snorts. *That wasn't right.*
Start over. So I do it again, tapping out the rhythm with my
fingers as I go, counting under my breath, *one, two, three,*
four, five, six . . . and then I do it again, and again, and
again, trying to get it to feel just right. The night deepens
around me, and my T-shirt is soaked through, but I keep at
it for what seems like hours.

Once, among the meager selection of books in our
school's dim, dusty library, Saf and I found a copy of an
illustrated *Sejarah Melayu*, a slim volume of fantastical
folktales and stories that supposedly captured the "glorious history of the Malays." Our favorite was the legend
of Hang Nadim, whose coastal village was cursed with
a plague of swordfish thanks, as always, to the actions
of a feckless, wretched king. The swordfish flew out of
the water in droves, piercing the bodies of the men and
women who had the misfortune to be by the sea that particular day. At first, the king—not the wisest fellow, you
see—ordered his men to stand shoulder to shoulder and
use their legs to prevent the swordfish from getting past.
But obviously all that did was result in the deaths of more
people, until Hang Nadim, bright lad that he was, thought

up the idea of using the soft stems of the banana tree as a barrier instead. The leaping swordfish found themselves stuck in the stems, no more men were sacrificed, and Hang Nadim was hailed as a hero by all except the king, who later ordered his execution. It doesn't do to expose your ruler's stupidity.

Saf and I would peal with laughter at the absurdity of this story, but in my heart I always felt a small ache for the men who stood on that beach and let themselves be pierced by hundreds of sharp objects flying straight at them from an unrelenting sea, all to protect their own.

This feels a lot like that. The Djinn hurls swordfish after swordfish at me, enjoying the sight of my skin being pierced by their sharp blades, my flesh being ripped apart, my weaknesses seeping through for all the world to see. But still I pace, and tap, and count. I need to protect my people.

Eventually, I have to stop, pushing the hair off my damp forehead impatiently. My eyes are so tired they feel like they're about to shrivel up and drop out of their sockets. *Getting sleepy?* The Djinn smiles charmingly. *I have some movies we can watch together, if you like?*

Shut up. I dig a nail into my left arm so hard that it leaves a deep red crescent on my pale skin. *Focus, Mel. Let's do this one more time.*

Just one more time.

CHAPTER EIGHT

VINCENT COMES HOME FROM HIS first day as a volunteer practically glowing with usefulness. "I was going crazy at home," he confesses to me as we wait for Auntie Bee to call us for dinner. "Just hanging around, not knowing what was happening. Now at least I know I'm helping. I'm not waiting around for something to happen."

"Any news of Kampung Baru?" I don't know why I ask, when I'm almost afraid to hear the answer. The Djinn summons lumps of cold fear from deep in my belly and lodges them in my throat, making it ache, making it hard for me to breathe.

He shakes his head, his expression apologetic. "I'm sorry, Mel," he says. "I wasn't in town today; I was sorting and packing supplies over in Keramat. I'm supposed to drive out tomorrow. I'll check for you then, okay? Maybe try and get a message to your mother?"

I can tell he wishes he could tell me something more, and I swallow my frustration. "Okay," I say.

He sits at his place at the table, so confident, so sure, so full of pride at what he's doing to help. His enthusiasm is seductive, contagious. But I'm not fooled. Beneath that assuredness, he's soft and vulnerable. They all are, I realize suddenly, staring around the table. I need to protect him. I need to protect them all.

The way you protected Saf? the Djinn whispers. *The way you're protecting Mama now, by staying here and saving your own skin?* In my head, the man in the theater laughs and laughs, and both Mama's and Saf's bodies lie broken at his feet. I pick up my spoon and tap it lightly on the edge of my bowl three times, then I stir three times clockwise, then three times counterclockwise, and then I do it all over again, trying very hard not to throw up all over the table.

"Was there any danger?" Auntie Bee asks him. She's been mostly silent throughout the meal; in fact, she's been mostly silent for the entire day while Vince was gone, throwing herself feverishly into her household tasks while I try to stay out of her way. I know what it's like when your brain takes one idea and decides to turn it into a feature-length film. Distraction is good.

Vince hesitates, and I can tell he's wondering exactly how much he should tell her. "It was fine," he says eventually, turning his attention back to his rice bowl so he doesn't have to meet her sharp, searching gaze. "Police and army guys everywhere, lots of roadblocks, so there can't really be any hanky-panky. They nip that stuff in the bud real quick. Plus, nobody hurts the volunteers." He shrugs. "Everybody's always happy to see us—Malays, Chinese, Indians, aunties, uncles, gangsters. Everyone needs food."

"Eh, can you stop that?" Frankie suddenly says loudly, and I freeze as everyone stares at me, my spoon still resting lightly on the bowl's rim. "We're trying to talk and you keep tapping on your bowl, *ding ding ding*, it's damn irritating."

Every eye on me feels like a laser boring straight into my body, and I can feel my face grow hot and tears sting my eyes, and I can't move. What do I do? What do I do? The Djinn's laughter echoes through my head. *Keep going and they'll know you're crazy. Stop and your mother dies. What a lovely little conundrum this is!*

Auntie Bee's voice cuts through his wicked hisses. "Girl," she says gently. "Girl, are you all right?"

I still can't move.

Beneath the table, I feel a hand on my knee, gentle, soothing. I glance at Vince, but he isn't looking at me. Instead, he moves quickly and somehow his other hand knocks over his glass so that it shatters on the floor, water and shards of glass flying everywhere.

Everyone leaps up in shock. "Aiya!" Auntie Bee cries as water begins to seep into the kitchen rug.

"Sorry, Ma," Vince says. "I don't know what happened."

"So clumsy," she scolds him, scurrying to the kitchen for a rag. "Quickly, Frankie, roll back that rug before it gets spoiled, then go and get some newspaper to wrap up this glass. Vincent, you go and get the broom and sweep up this mess. Nobody step on any pieces lah, you will cut your feet to ribbons!"

Through this chaos, Uncle Chong sits calmly finishing up the last of his porridge as if nothing is happening, and when I tap my spoon lightly on the side of my bowl—*ding, ding, ding*—nobody notices at all.

"Take me with you."

"Huh?" Vince looks up at me from where he lies sprawled among his records on the floor. He's just put on a Bee Gees record—"The First of May," a somber cut soaked in longing for times gone by that always leaves me feeling sad and hollow.

I say it again, louder this time. "Take me with you."

He sits up slowly and stops the record player. "Why?" he asks. "Why would I do that?"

"I want to help too," I tell him. "I can't stay here doing nothing. I need to know where my mother is, need to find out what happened to her, if she's okay. If I go out with you, then maybe I can ask around, figure it out." *If*

I find her, then I can protect her. And if I'm with you, I can protect you. It's not a lie; it's just not the whole truth.

He sighs. "I know. But it isn't safe out there."

"But you told your mother—"

"Of course I told my mother it was safe! You think she'd let me go if she knew what it was really like out there?" He snorts. "Not bloody likely."

"So what's it really like?"

He hesitates. "Pretty much how I imagined it," he says finally, and I roll my eyes. I know an evasion when I see one; I'm usually the one using it.

"So you were in danger?"

"Mel, anyone who steps out their doors right now is in danger. I can't let you do it."

"If you don't let me come with you, I'll have to go on my own," I point out reasonably. "Then you wouldn't know where I was or if I was protected. Whereas if you were with me . . ." I trail off, letting the infinite probabilities unfold in his head.

It doesn't take long. I can tell by his scowl that I've won and he knows it.

"Fine," he growls. "But you'll have to explain to Ma. And you'll have to put up with Jagdev."

"Who's Jagdev?"

"You'll see."

• • •

Jagdev turns out to be a large Sikh man with a belly that hangs over the waistband of his khakis and a beard that can only be described as luxuriant. When he laughs—which he does often, usually at jokes the rest of us don't really get—his eyes crease up into a dozen tiny crinkles, and his turban wobbles so that I am half willing it to come off and half worried that it will.

"Welcome to the gang!" he bellows, chuckling to himself as he holds open the door of his ancient black car for me. "You can call me Jay!"

"Thanks, Jay," I mutter, sliding onto the worn leather seats, torn and patched in places. My eyes are swollen, and I feel strangely light, like I may float off into the sky at any minute. I've barely slept, having spent the night pacing Vince's room in a special series of patterns and sequences designed to placate the Djinn and protect the entire house while I'm gone. Each time I tried to sleep, I'd close my eyes and watch Auntie Bee and Uncle Chong die, again and again. Then I'd get up, shaken and nauseous, and do it all over again, until light began to stream through the window and I realized it was morning.

They think Vince and Jay are taking me to an aunt's house in Sungai Buloh. "Thank you for letting me stay for so long, but I need to be with family right now," I'd reassured them. "I'll be safe with them." The tears that slide down my cheeks are real; I don't want to leave this family that took me in so easily, that practices kindness like a religion. But it's the only way.

I see them exchange worried glances, but they agree, and I feel a sharp pang at how easily this deception comes to me, and how easily it is received. *It's not a total lie*, I tell myself. I do have an aunt in Sungai Buloh—mad Auntie Jun. "So thin, how to get any boys like this!" she likes to shriek whenever she sees me, poking me in my ribs. We haven't actually seen Auntie Jun in the past year—she has a daughter around my age, my cousin Nora, and doesn't want her tainted by my own peculiar brand of madness— but Auntie Bee and Uncle Chong don't need to know that.

While Jay and Vince catch up, I occupy myself con- structing an intricate web of numbers and taps, weaving a protective shell around the whole car, around Vincent and Jay and me. Three taps at a time here, here, here, and here, now the feet, now the fingers, and again. Once or twice, I feel like I'm being watched, like Vincent is eyeing me in the rearview mirror. But every time I look up, his eyes are either firmly on the road ahead, or on Jay as they talk and laugh in the front seat. *You're imagining things, Melati.*

Oh, yes? The Djinn tickles my heart gently, sending cold shoots of anxiety spiraling through my chest. *But what if he did? Think how shameful it would be for him to see you acting this way. How utterly disgusted he would be to know they opened their home to someone like you.* I feel my cheeks heat up. *Begin again.* So I do, tapping and counting, concentrating hard until the world fades into numbers and nothing more.

"Where are we going?" I finally ask over the roar and rumble of the engine once I'm satisfied. It's a hot day; Jay and Vince roll down their windows so that the wind whips my hair about and stings my eyes. "Klang," Jay booms back. "Got a tip. This man said he abandoned his lorry full of fresh eggs there when the troubles started. Says we can have the eggs to distribute if we just return the lorry to him in good condition. Or should I say, egg-cellent condition. Ha!"

I smile weakly. Vince groans, then looks back and catches my eye. "Brace yourself," he says quietly. I'm about to ask him what for, when I look out of the window and see Kuala Lumpur for myself, for the first time since it all began.

The streets are desolate. The walls of the empty shop-houses bear the bruises of their recent altercations: spattered trails of blood and bullet holes, a map of senseless violence. Here, the smoldering husk of a burned-out car; there, a smattering of broken glass from shop windows; farther on, a sprawling stain on the pavement roughly the shape of Australia that couldn't be mistaken for anything other than dried blood. And a sight that seems oddly familiar, though for a second I don't realize it's because

I'm so used to seeing them in my head: limp, lifeless bodies, more than I can count. Men, women, and even children, some who look around my age, some even younger, some still wearing their school uniforms. One girl's blue ribbon trails behind her on the pavement where she lies, intertwined with the hair that's come loose from her half-undone braid.

That girl could have been just like me and Saf, I think, *walking back from school, talking about boys and records and movies, secure in the belief that teenagers like us aren't meant to be personally acquainted with death until some hazy, far-off day in the future, when we're old and gray.*

And then the Djinn whispers: *Maybe one of those bodies IS Saf.*

And then: *Maybe one of them is Mama.*

And then I cannot breathe.

As I count and tap and tap and count, my fingers shaking, the Djinn's soft rasp ever-present in my ear, I hear Jay let out a long sigh. "Bloody politicians," he says softly, shaking his head. "Bloody politicians and their bloody stupid rhetoric, speeches, ideologies. You ever hear anyone say words don't matter after this, you tell them about this day, when Malay idiots and Chinese idiots decided to kill one another because they believed what the bloody politicians told them."

I want more than anything to close my eyes, to say something, tell them to turn back and send me home, tell them I wasn't meant for this, that nobody was meant for this. But the Djinn reaches out his cold, bony fingers and forces my eyelids open. *Take it all in*, he hisses. *You wanted to be out here. You wanted to be the hero, the protector. You wanted to see what was happening for yourself. So see.*

My breath is coming in short, shallow pants, and my hands are trembling uncontrollably. Every body that I see bears Mama's face. *She's dead*, says the voice in my head. *You left her. You failed her, just like you failed Saf. And now she's dead.* I fight to quash him, force him down, keep him silent, but the effort is making me queasy. I'm going to throw up, I think. I'm going to throw up.

"I'm going to throw up," I say quickly. Jay brings the car to a screeching halt, and I open the door just in time, heaving up the morning's meager breakfast—boiled sweet potatoes, again. I feel almost detached as it happens, as though I'm floating outside my own body, watching it enthusiastically expel lumpy, pale yellow liquid.

What an idiot.

"Are you okay?" Vince asks, frowning with concern. "I should have known—it's a lot to take in." I am flushed and embarrassed when I sit back up, and Jay silently passes me his large cotton handkerchief. "Thank you," I say quietly, wiping my mouth with it. The initials JS are embroidered neatly in one corner in navy-blue thread. For some reason, this makes me want to cry.

"*JS* for Jagdev Singh," he says, following the direction of my gaze. "Although when my wife is angry with me, she says it stands for Jolly Stupid!" I laugh then, and suddenly feel better.

"I don't suppose you want this back. . . ."

He looks at the crumpled square in my hand and grimaces. "You keep it," he says. "I have plenty more."

"Let's go," Vince says, looking up and down the street. "We have some eggs to collect."

"How egg-citing!" Jay says, grinning.

"How long is this going to go on, Jagdev?" Vince asks him.

"I dunno, Vince, I think some jokes are egg-xactly what we need right now," I tell him, and Jay laughs delightedly as we make our way toward Klang.

As we drive on, we pass shiny red trucks laden with men in blue-and-red uniforms bearing stout truncheons—"FRU," Jay explains to me. "Federal Reserve Unit, the riot police"— and roadblocks staffed by armed guards who demand our credentials. Each time, Vince shows them the curfew pass, and we're waved on. Once, we are asked to submit to a search of the vehicle, so we stand by patiently and I count off the seconds in my head as an overzealous army officer pokes among our bags of rice, medical supplies, and other provisions, hoping, I suppose, to unearth secret weapons.

"Do you have to do that? We're just taking food to people who need it," says Vince. "Can't be too careful," the young man says, flashing us a grin. "We need to make sure you aren't a danger. We are here to protect the people." And he sticks his bayonet right into a bag, piercing it through so that rice spills from the jagged tear, all over the floor of Jay's car.

On my right, a sharp intake of breath from Jay, though he doesn't say a word; on my left, Vince narrows his eyes and I can tell how furious he is. It's difficult not to be. Times are scarce, and one bag of rice could get a family or two through many a long hard week.

Finally, after sixty-seven sets of three and at least two scenarios where my mother has died excruciating deaths, we're told to load our things back up and move on. "All clear," the man says, with another grin and a thumbs-up.

"Thank you," Vince says.

The man looks at him. "Thank you, *sir*," he says.

Vincent takes in a sharp breath, and I bite my bottom lip so hard I taste blood.

"Thank you, *sir*."

When we finally reach Klang, we have no problem finding the abandoned lorry exactly where the owner says he left it. By some miracle, not a single egg inside it is smashed. "Everyone we meet is going to be so egg-static to see these," Jay says, and even Vince cracks a smile. He hasn't spoken a word since we left the roadblock.

We split up then, the better to get supplies to more people. We divide the spoils, Jay taking the lorry, Vince taking over driving duties in the car, and me sliding into the front seat to keep him company. Our next stop, he tells me, is a row of houses near Sentul.

When we arrive at the first home, we're greeted with glad cries by the occupants: a young Indian woman who says her name is Mala, and her white-haired mother, wrapped in a shabby green sari. "I'm so glad you are here," Mala says, clapping her hands at the sight of the rice and the eggs we bring to her door. "We need your help. Please come inside."

Vince and I trade glances. "Of course, ma'am," he says politely. As we follow behind her, he leans in. "Be careful, and stay close to me."

Inside, a man lays sprawled on a mat on the floor, the back of his head sporting a large bandage. He sits up when he sees us, eyes wild and poised to flee, or attack—I can't tell which. "It's all right, Roslan," Mala says gently, and he calms at the sound of her voice.

"He was running away," she explains to us. "He tripped right in front of our house and banged his head against a rock. I was peeping out the window and saw him. So I quickly pulled him inside before anyone could see him."

I smile. "You are very kind."

She dips her head gracefully, too shy to acknowledge the compliment. "The thing is, he doesn't want to stay here. He wants to go home."

"Please," the man says, his voice hoarse. "Please. I'd like to go home to my family."

"All right," Vince says slowly. "So what's the problem?"

Mala clears her throat. "The problem is that Roslan lives in Segambut. He's worried that he'll be hurt on the way from here to there." She catches my eye. "There are a lot of . . . unfriendly . . . areas for him to pass by."

Vince catches on faster than I do. "Chinese areas?" he says.

"Areas that may not be . . . as friendly toward a big Malay man walking on his own."

There is a silence as we all take this in. Roslan trembles, and Mala's mother totters to the kitchen, returning with a cup of hot tea. She sits beside him on the floor, stroking his back softly while he sips at it. The green and gold threads of her sari shimmer as she moves.

And that's when it hits me.

"A sari," I say aloud. "We need a sari."

"What?" Vince looks at me like I've sprouted horns.

"We could dress him in a sari. I mean, look at him." Everyone turns to look, and Roslan shrinks a little from the weight of our gazes. "He's dark—tall, but not impossibly tall for a woman. He can drape the shawl over his head so nobody sees his bandage. And if he rides in the back with them"—I gesture at the two women—"it'll look like we're just driving a group of Indian ladies somewhere. No Malays in sight."

Another silence as everyone considers this plan. On the floor, Roslan's eyes blaze with hope.

"It could work," Mala says eventually. "It really could."

Vince shrugs. "What do we have to lose?"

And Mala's mother grins a gap-toothed grin as she scurries off to find the perfect sari.

Half an hour later, Roslan stands in the middle of the room, his arms outstretched, as Mala and her mother put the finishing touches to his outfit. He's draped in a bright blue sari, shot with threads of gold that gleam against his dark skin.

"It works," Vince says, standing back to take in the full effect.

"Good," Roslan says, sighing with relief. "Now let's go." He starts for the door, then freezes when we all yell, "Stop!"

"What?" he says, wide-eyed.

Vince shakes his head. "You won't get more than five steps before someone figures out you aren't a woman," he says. "Your walk is a dead giveaway."

"What's wrong with the way I walk?"

"Nothing," I say soothingly. "It's very manly. But that's the problem."

"You need to be a little more . . . fluid," Mala says. "Roll your hips a little bit. Like this." She walks across the room gracefully, a stark contrast to Roslan's wide strides.

He clicks his tongue impatiently. "Must I really do this?"

"Look, do you want to make it home or not?" I ask him.

He sighs, but eventually submits to a fifteen-minute walking lesson, trying so hard to move the right way that by the time we finish, sweat is streaming down his face.

"All right," Mala says, "I think that's the best we can do."

A shadow of doubt falls across Roslan's face. "Do you really think this will work?" he says, tugging absently at the soft material that swirls down to his ankles. Mala's mother reaches out a wizened hand to pat his. "You will be okay," she says softly.

Roslan takes a deep breath. "All right," he says. "I'm ready."

The car is silent on the drive from Sentul to Segambut. "It should take us about fifteen minutes to get there," Vince tells us, but it feels like every inch the car moves forward ages us all by about ten years. "Hurry, hurry," Mala mutters under her breath. Roslan says nothing at all; he just sits sandwiched between the two women, one hand holding tight to Mala's mother's, the other clutching at the shawl on his head.

"We're almost there," Vince announces, and I'm about to let out a joyous whoop when I see something that makes my heart stop.

A roadblock.

From the back seat, I hear a sharp intake of breath from Mala.

"What do we do?" she whispers.

I feel a churning in my stomach; slowly, the Djinn begins to stir.

"Just act natural," Vince says calmly. "Let me do the talking."

The car rolls to a stop next to the young Malay soldier manning the barricade, who nods at Vince. "Pass, please," he says, and Vince hands over his curfew pass for inspection. The young man frowns slightly as he looks over the paper, and the Djinn squeezes my heart in response. *You're all in trouble now*, he whispers.

"Where are you headed?" the soldier asks.

"Just getting these ladies back to their home in Segambut," Vince replies easily. I steal a glance over my shoulder at the trio behind me; in Mala's eyes, I see a mirror for my own mute panic. The only movement in the back seat is the trembling of Roslan's hands.

Still holding Vince's pass, the soldier peers into the car,

taking a long look first at me, then at the others in the back. I can't tell from his gaze what he's thinking, and my uncertainty is fodder for the Djinn, who cackles softly and parades a dozen images of our deaths through my head in quick succession.

Finally, *finally*, the soldier hands the pass back through the window. "All right, go ahead," he tells Vince. "Mind you get home quickly; it does no good to be wandering about too late right now."

"Yes, sir. Thank you, sir." Vince eases the car back onto the road to Segambut.

Five seconds later, we all burst out into hysterical, wild laughter.

The bright afternoon sun gives way to a mellower golden glow, and after sending Mala and her mother back to their house, Vince decides it's time for us to head home. "We'll tell Ma we couldn't make it to Sungai Buloh," he says. "We'll have to try again tomorrow."

"Okay," I say agreeably. I'm breathless, euphoric: From somewhere in the depths of my chaotic, broken brain, I had produced a good idea. A good idea. Me! And we'd actually pulled it off, and gotten a man back to his home, and it was because of ME. As someone who has spent so much time in the past weeks and months feeling like I need saving, I am almost dizzy with the realization that I can also be someone who saves other people.

Can you? The Djinn's voice is like smoke, snaking through my brain. *Can you really? What did you do but provide one idea? Who actually had to carry it out?* And then, crushingly: *If you think you're so capable of saving people, then why didn't you?* In my head, Saf and Mama bleed rivers of bright red through fresh gunshot wounds, the edges ragged from where bullet holes tore through their flesh. I inhale sharply and close my eyes, trying to ignore him, trying to hold on to that feeling of triumph, trying to stop my twitching fingers from flying to do his bidding. And I almost succeed.

Until Vince leans forward to squint at the road ahead. "What's that?"

I sit up to take a better look. "What?"

"That thing there, in the middle of the road."

We're getting closer and closer, and it's clear that whatever it is, we're not going to be able to get past. He eases the car to a stop. "Wait here," he tells me, opening the door. "I'm going to see what that is. It's madness to have something blocking the road at a time like this."

I perch on the edge of my seat, watching him. The Djinn flutters his fingers lightly against the walls of my stomach, but I tamp him down. *I am the one who saves,* I tell him firmly, *not the one who needs saving.*

Vince walks a little way down the road from the car,

peering at the offending blockade, then looks back at me. "It's just a tree trunk! I'm going to . . ."

"Going to what?" I yell back. Then I realize he's gone perfectly still, and that his eyes are wide and staring at something right behind me. My stomach immediately clenches in fear. Before I can look around, he's sprinted back to the car and leaped into the driver's seat, slamming the door behind him. In what feels like no time at all, he's swerved the car back around so fast that the tires screech in protest, then slams on the accelerator like we're being chased by hellhounds. I can't help the frightened yelp that escapes me, or keep myself from gripping the door handle so hard I leave permanent nail marks in the worn leather. "What is going on?!" I yell over the rumbling of the engine, which is working harder than it probably has in its whole life. Vince doesn't answer; he just keeps driving like a maniac, shooting periodic glances at his rearview mirror.

Finally, after a full fifteen minutes of heart-pounding racing in which all I do is count and tap in small clusters of three, he slows to something resembling normal speed, and I take a minute to catch my breath. "What was that all about?" I shout at him.

He takes a deep breath. His face, I realize, is deathly pale. "That thing in the middle of the road," he says. "It was part of a tree trunk—a banana tree, I think."

"That was it? It must have just fallen over or something." He's still, quiet. "You're not worried about Pontianaks, are you?" I tease him, hoping for a smile, a laugh, anything to break him out of this strange mood. My mother used to tell me stories from her own grandmother, about the blood-sucking Pontianaks, demon women who lived in banana trees and came back from the dead to snatch innocent babies from unsuspecting new mothers. "And if you're naughty, I'll tell her to come and take you, too!" she'd say, smacking me lightly on my bottom while I giggled, immersing myself in the delicious terror of it all.

"It didn't just fall over," he says finally. "No jagged edges like you get on a broken trunk. Someone cut it down and put it there."

I frown. "Who would do something like that?"

"People up to no good," he says, smiling wanly. "The people I saw coming up behind the car, for example."

"What?!"

He nods. "That's what I saw when I looked back. That's what made me panic. They were creeping out from behind those clusters of trees and bushes by the side of the road. They had weapons. . . . It was a trap."

My hands are shaking, and I clench them into fists to try and get them to stop. "But . . . but . . . Who were they even trying to catch in that trap? Us? It doesn't make sense." My breath is coming hard and fast now, and I can hear my voice rising, tinged with hysteria. "We were only there to help!"

"I don't think they cared, Melati," says Vince, his voice gentle. "I think that people are angry and frustrated, and they just want to lash out and hurt someone. It doesn't really matter who."

"That's crazy!"

"It's just the truth. They don't see us as people, and they don't want to. They just know that we're not them. That's enough."

My breathing is so ragged and uneven I'm starting to see black spots in front of my eyes. I shut them tight, and immediately see Mama being bashed over the head with an iron pipe. *Not one of us*, says the faceless man standing over her body as he shrugs, blood dripping down his wrist and landing on the ground before him. Without even thinking, I start to count, my fingers tapping convulsively—one, two, three, one, two, three—but the image won't go away. Why won't it go away? I can't breathe, I swear, I can't breathe. Again and again, Mama dies right in front of my eyes, and there's nothing, nothing, nothing that I can do about it. *Count, Melati, damn you, count or she'll die. One, two, three, one, two, three, one, two, three* . . . Vincent, the tree trunk, the men and their weapons, Mama covered in her own blood—the whole world fades away until there's nothing left but me and the numbers.

• • •

"Why do you do that?"

My eyes fly open and I see Vincent looking at me. "Do what?" I say, my heart beating so hard I swear you can see it bouncing out of my chest, like some kind of cartoon character. How long have I been sitting here like this? How long has he been watching me? A dark shame begins to blossom from the pit of my stomach.

"Your fingers—they never stop. And I can hear you counting sometimes, under your breath. What are you counting?"

My face burns icy hot; my toes curl in agony. I let him see me. How could I let him see me? For one wild moment I consider lying, thinking up some story, anything to put him off the scent. But I'm tired of lying, of hiding all the time, of pretending everything is fine. The numbers are wearing me down. I'm sick of it. The Djinn courses wildly through my body, screeching as he senses my impending betrayal.

How do I even begin?

Okay, Melati. Deep breath.

"So . . . imagine your mind is a house. You fill it with things and people and ideas and thoughts that are important to you and worth keeping, right?" He nods, not wanting to interrupt. "Well, in my house, the back door sometimes opens all by itself, and uninvited people just let themselves in and get comfortable. They talk really loudly, they do whatever they want, and they never seem to want to leave."

So far, so good. I keep going.

"Those strangers in my house . . . they aren't really me. But because they act like they own the place, sometimes it's hard to tell if what I'm thinking is really . . . what I'm thinking, if that makes sense."

"Okay . . ."

I can hear the hesitation in his voice, and it almost makes me falter. In my head, the Djinn replays the memory of my mother's recoil when I told her my truth, over and over and over again.

"When I get stressed, when I get worried, when I find myself thinking about something that I don't want in my head, I sort of . . . count things. To help me calm down." I glance over at him to see how he's taking this.

"Does it work?" he asks.

"Sure. Well. Most of the time." *Stop,* the Djinn whispers. *Stop. He'll hate you for saying any more.* I ignore him and forge on. "I can't just count any which way. I have to count in threes."

"Threes?"

I nod. "Yeah. That's the magic number. So everything I count has to be in threes, or the total has to be a number that can be divided by three. Or if there's a bunch of things, I can only count every third thing. Sometimes I count words in books, or things people say, or the steps that I take. Sometimes I have to touch things when I count them, or sometimes I have to tap out my count—like with my fingers, or my feet. . . ." My voice trails off. This is too weird. Even saying it, I know it sounds too weird. He's about to call me crazy, call a doctor, call a bomoh.

Instead, he just asks: "Why three?"

I shoot him a look. He actually seems interested. "I don't know," I say honestly. "I've thought about it a lot, and I think maybe it's because the last time I was happy, the last time my mind was quiet, it was when we were the three of us. You know. A proper family."

There. It's all out. Well, almost all of it—I can't quite bring myself to tell him about the Djinn, but even then, I'm new to this being-honest-about-my-mental-and-emotional-state thing, and this is enough. I feel a strange combination of exhaustion, relief, and utter vulnerability, as though I'm naked next to him. Baby steps.

This pause is stretching on for far too long now, and I'm aching to look at him, search his face for clues, ask him flat out what he's thinking.

Don't look. Don't look, Melati.

The tips of my ears burn, and I rub them self-consciously as I wait for him to respond.

"That sounds exhausting." I strain my ears for any

hint of disgust or pity, but amazingly enough, all I hear in his voice is compassion.

"It is."

"Is there anything that makes it better?"

I think about this for a while, trying to find the right words. "Music," I say, finally. "Music calms me down. For my last birthday before my father . . . before he . . . you know. Before he died—" The word sticks in my throat, but I forge on. "They bought me my own record player. And even though my mom can't really afford it now that it's the two of us, every other month she somehow scrapes together the money to buy me a new record."

The memory of it brings up fresh tears: Mama and me at the record store, flipping through the latest releases, giggling over particularly garish album covers, shrieking with excitement when we find the perfect one.

"She sounds like an amazing woman," Vince says softly.

"She was. I mean, is," I quickly correct myself. *Djinn got your tongue?* the voice purrs, and not for the first time, I wish I could strangle him. I look down at my lap dreamily and realize that I've been tapping and counting the entire time. Quickly, I stuff my fingers beneath me and hope Vince didn't notice.

"The thing about a song is that, if you break it down,

it's all chaos," I say. "Like, there's all these different notes, different instruments, different sounds. It's a mess. But you add a beat and a rhythm and somehow everything can come together and make something beautiful. I think that's what I'm trying to do. Find a rhythm for the mess in my head, so that it somehow . . . makes sense."

I steal another glance at him; he's looking straight ahead as he drives, frowning a little. I can tell he's thinking about everything I've told him. The silence stretches on and on, and I can feel that familiar flutter. The Djinn opens his palms and releases a thousand tiny black birds, all flapping their wings frantically against the walls of my stomach. *He thinks you're crazy. He thinks you're crazy. He thinks you're crazy.* My palms start to sweat, and before I realize it, my fingers have worked their way back onto my lap and are moving as if they have minds of their own. I close my eyes. *One, two, three, one, two, three, one, two, three, one, two . . .*

My mind stutters to a stop. I open my eyes.

Vincent has reached over and taken my hand firmly in his, lacing our fingers together so mine can no longer tap out their endless refrain.

No boy has ever held my hand before.

Before I can say a word, he starts to sing a familiar song. "Little darling," he calls me, his voice cracking on the unaccustomed high notes. "Little darling," and my heart begins to melt.

He's not very good, and I want to laugh, even though I can feel tears pooling in my eyes. *Don't cry, stupid!* I tell myself firmly. *Don't cry!* So instead, I sing along, and our voices soar and blend together as we tell ourselves over and over again what we so desperately want to believe: Here comes the sun.

CHAPTER NINE

"AGAIN?" AUNTIE BEE STARES AT me aghast, her mouth open in a perfect O of dismay. "You are going with them AGAIN?"

"Yes, Auntie." I nod, not quite able to look her in the eye.

"We had to come home yesterday, Ma," Vince steps in. "By the time I finished the deliveries, there wasn't any time left to go to Sungai Buloh before it got dark. We'll make it there this time. Melati needs to be with her family," he adds virtuously.

Auntie Bee isn't happy, and if I'm honest, I'm not in a huge hurry to get back out there either. Vince might have distracted me momentarily on that drive home, but in the night, my demon came back to plague me in a rampaging fury. I've spent my night fighting off the deaths of all the people I care about, and today I feel like I'm looking at the world through a thick, dense fog.

All I want to do is lie in bed and sleep forever.

Stop it, you weakling, I tell myself sternly. *You can't do this. Not today.* Vince has promised me that we'll make it to Kampung Baru today no matter what. I'm dressed in my own clothes this time, my white blouse and turquoise pinafore clean and dry now, my backpack slung over my shoulders, my hair tied back in a neat ponytail. Auntie Bee offers more of her niece's clothes, but I refuse. Today is the day I'm going to finally, finally see my mother and make sure she's really, truly okay. If I'm going to wage battle with demons both on the street and in my own head, I'm going to do it with all of myself, and not weighed down by borrowed clothes and secondhand memories.

Auntie Bee sighs, rubbing the bridge of her nose with her finger and thumb. "Fine, fine," she mutters. "Don't listen to me, what do I know? I'm just an old woman who doesn't want to outlive her children. Tell me, is that too much to ask?"

Vince grins and hugs her. "So dramatic, Ma. You're not in some Chinese soap opera, you know."

She doesn't even crack a smile. "Every minute you are gone, I age a year, you know that?" she tells him seriously. "Better come back faster, before I use up all my years waiting for you."

We hear the distinctive toot of Jay's horn outside, and Vince immediately heads for the door. I hang back. I want to reassure Auntie Bee somehow, tell her we'll be fine. Instead, I find myself reaching for her hands. She stares at me, surprised, as I take them in mine and bend low over them, touching my lips to the soft, papery skin. It's the same good-bye I give my mother whenever I leave the house. "He'll be back soon, Auntie," I say. "Try not to worry too much." Then I dash for the car, pretending I don't see her eyes mist over with tears.

The boys are waiting for me in the front seat as I open the back door and slide in, dropping my backpack on the floor. "Typical girl, keeping us waiting like this," Jay says, wagging a finger at me.

"Typical man, expecting every girl to come as soon as he calls, like a good dog," I shoot back, and he laughs.

"All right, today we're heading toward Kampung Baru," Vince says, taking charge. "That's the area that's worst hit, they say. We'll try to get to some places before then, but I think we'll mostly be concentrating on drop-offs along Batu Road."

Jay snaps off a jaunty salute. "Okay, boss!"

"Okay, boss!" I say, following suit. In my head, I've already begun the work of securing the car, making it safe for all of us.

Vince shoots a glance at me over his shoulder, then turns back to survey the road before us. "Say, Jay, you feel like singing?" he says. I look down at my fingers, twisting anxiously in my lap, and smile. I know what he's doing.

"Singing?"

"Yes, singing! What songs do you like?"

Jay thinks about this for a second. "I don't know, really," he muses. "All you young people, your music just gives me a headache."

"Okay, then, let's sing something you know. Something happy."

"What nonsense is this? Why must we sing?"

"Come on, Jay . . . ," Vince wheedles. "It'll make the ride go by much faster, you'll see."

It takes a few minutes of back-and-forth, but in the end Jay gives in, launching into a spirited rendition of "Twist and Shout." "The Beatles!" I crow happily, and he stops to look at me, scandalized. "The Beatles! Those mop-haired delinquents? No, no, this is the great Chuck Berry!"

"What does it matter?" Vince grins. "It's a great song!"

Jay starts singing then, almost howling the words, grinding out some awkward dance moves behind the wheel as Vince puckers his lips and shimmies in his seat in his role as principal backup singer, and all I can do is laugh so hard I think I may throw up again.

Jay is in the middle of growling out the second verse when I realize that Vince's voice has trailed off. The happy bubble we've encased ourselves in shimmers, then bursts altogether, and the air that comes rushing in is thick with tension. "Stop," Vince says, his voice ringing with authority. Jay pulls the car into a parking space. "Stay here," Vince tells me, ignoring my outraged expression, then "Come on," to Jay, and they both head out and down to the riverbank.

Stay here? We'll see about that, I think. So I get out of the car too.

Floating lazily in the water, swaying with the current, are bodies.

Part of me wants to retch; another part of me notes once again how familiar this scene is to my visions, this tableau of death and gore brought to life; one final other part, the one the Djinn has a firm grasp on, notes with grim satisfaction that there are six bodies, two sets of three, a safe number (although not, obviously, for them). Some are on their backs, their faces turned toward the sky; some are on their fronts, staring into the dark depths of the river. One is a girl who, I presume from the turquoise pinafore just like the one I'm wearing, is around my age. I'm glad she's facedown; I don't think I can bear to see her expression.

Instead, I look at Vince, whose mouth is set in a tight, thin line. "We have to get them out," he tells Jay. "We can't just leave them there." The older man just nods. All traces of laughter have been sucked out of him; he looks beaten, deflated.

They begin looking around them, scouring the ground for long sticks they can use to poke and prod and fish the bodies out of the water, and suddenly I can't bear to watch.

"I'll be in the car," I mumble, stumbling over my own feet as I scramble up the riverbank. *That could have been me*, I think, remembering the girl in the school uniform. *That could have been me.* And then, almost immediately: *That could be Mama.*

There it is, that familiar creeping doubt. None of those bodies was Mama. *But are you sure? Did you check? Did you see all of their faces? Or did you run away, like the coward you are, like you did on the day you let your best friend die?*

I clench my fists, feeling the Djinn start to rise, his dark shadow unfurling like smoke from somewhere deep within my belly and spreading through my entire body. *No, no, please, no.* I'm so tired that the idea of giving in to the numbers makes me scratchy and irritable. I want to cry. But I can't keep thinking about this, and I can't keep seeing those images burned behind my eyelids, and my skin is starting to feel tight, like I'm wearing a buttoned-up coat two sizes too small, and so I count and count and count and count. I try to count the number of leaves on the big angsana tree shading the car from the morning sun, but the outstretched branches quiver in the wind, and I keep worrying that I've missed one, which makes me

panicky. So instead, I think about the word "angsana"—
ang-sa-na, three syllables, so that's safe, but it's seven letters, which isn't. How to neutralize it? I add the letters
in "tree," which brings it up to eleven. Still not safe. The
word for "tree" in Malay is "pokok," and "pokok angsana" is twelve letters, which makes it safe. Good. What
else? I count the number of cracks and holes in the leather
seats of Jagdev's car—twenty-eight, not a good number;
I use my nail to make two tiny nicks so that I can make
it an even, perfect thirty and pray Jay never finds out. I
tap that number on the streaky windowpane, then tap it
again with my feet, alternating right and left. And all the
while, the Djinn holds me almost tenderly in his arms,
and laughs and laughs.

When the men finally return, they're rumpled and ashen
and I can't stomach asking them how they did it, or what
they did with the bodies. Instead, we ride on to Kampung
Baru without saying a word, the silence punctuated only
by the coughs and splutters of Jay's ancient car.

As we turn the corner onto Batu Road, I can't help but
sit up a little straighter, eager to catch a glimpse of home.

Or what's left of it.

Thick columns of black, black smoke rise from both
sides of Batu Road. Here, even the buildings bear scars of
the past week: broken windows, the haphazard patterns of

bullet holes, angry smoke stains, smoldering husks of what used to be shops and homes.

"They say this place was hit the hardest," Jay says, finally breaking the silence.

Vince shrugs. "It makes sense," he says. "On one side of Batu Road, Chow Kit, full of Chinese people and the triad members that protect them. On the other side, Kampung Baru, the biggest Malay village in town, protected by Alang and his goons. If you want to start an explosion, you light a match in the dynamite factory."

I can hear them, but their voices sound like they're coming from very far away, through a thick fog. I can't stop staring out of the window, at everything at once familiar and incredibly alien. Were these really the streets I'd walked only a few days ago? Everywhere I look, I see ghosts: Mel and Saf, walking arm in arm to the sundry shop with a list of provisions for our mothers; sucking on ais kepal in the heat of a Sunday afternoon, fingers tingling from holding on to the balls of shaved ice doused liberally in rose syrup; giggling about something in particular or nothing at all as we walk to the religious teacher's house for our weekly Quran-reading lessons. Or here and there, Mama, walking out in her brand-new kebaya with its fine lace-edged top and intricately patterned batik sarong, ready for Eid celebrations; Mama with a basket in hand, gabbing with the neighbor aunties on her way to market;

Mama tending to her garden, hose in hand. Mama. *It's all right*, I tell myself, trying to tamp down the jarring feeling of foreboding, the sense of impending doom. *It's all right. I'm home. Mama will be here. Everything will be all right. Mama will be here.*

"Mel?"

Vince's voice breaks the spell; I turn from the window to look at him, but my vision seems to blur for a second and it takes a while for my eyes to focus on his face. I suddenly feel exhausted.

"What do you want us to do now?" he asks.

I take in a deep breath, hold for a count of three, exhale. "Stop here," I say, gesturing to a clearing up ahead. "Let's see what we can find."

I don't know what I imagined I'd see when I got here. If I were honest, I'd admit that I had visions of Mama throwing open the doors to welcome me home, taking me in her arms in the tightest hug, never letting me go again.

Instead, here we are. My home, Mama's and mine, is a pile of blackened ash and rubble, and the houses that used to surround us aren't much better.

I can sense Vincent's eyes on me as he stands a little way away, giving me space, time to take it all in; Jay is waiting by the car. I walk through the detritus and although I feel like weeping, a part of me is fascinated by what the flames chose to consume and what they chose to keep intact: Our kitchen is completely devastated, but just steps away, our outhouse still proudly stands, all on its own; my prized records have been melted down into warped, unsalvageable lumps, but Mama's black-and-gold sewing machine stands untouched on its little table, the silver letters spelling out SINGER still visible under a layer of soot.

Mama. A fresh surge of panic rushes through me all at once, almost knocking me off my feet. Was Mama in the house when this happened? Did she make it out alive? I look around wildly; someone must know. Someone must know what happened to her.

Then I hear a woman's voice calling my name.

"Mama?" I whirl around, the ashes crunching beneath my feet. "Mama?" But no Mama answers my call. Instead, approaching me from a distance is Mak Siti, as neat and trim as ever, her hair tied back in a loose bun, her floral cotton baju kurung with nary a smidge of dirt besmirching it.

"Hello, Melati," she says, as though we're just making small talk at the market stand.

"Hello, Mak Siti," I say back, because what else am I supposed to say?

"I was waiting for you to come home from school, you know, the other day," she says, squinting at me. "Had dinner waiting. I took out a whole fish for you, fried it and everything. Your mother told me you were supposed to be home by four. Where were you, hmm?"

Is she seriously scolding me for not coming home on time on the day of a massive, bloody racial riot, in the middle of the charred ruins of my former home? Seriously? I look closely for any signs that she's kidding.

Oh. She isn't. Okay, then.

"Sorry, Mak Siti," I say, in the absence of any other alternative. This is becoming more and more surreal.

"Naughty, naughty," she tuts, pursing her lips. "Made me worry to death, once that nonsense started. I didn't know what I was supposed to tell your mother when she came home. Not to mention the waste! One whole fish, did I tell you? Those things aren't cheap, you know."

My heart lifts at the mention of my mother. "Mama! You saw Mama? Where is she? Is she—"

"Of course I saw your mama," Mak Siti interrupts, regarding my outburst with disapproval. "She came home early from her shift to look for you, make sure you were safe. Imagine how embarrassed I was when I had to tell her I didn't know where you were! I didn't know where to put my face! And the look on her! So much heartache you caused, young lady."

"Sorry, Mak Siti," I say again, because I can see that she expects it. "But do you know where Mama is now? Is she here? I need to see her."

She sniffs. "She's not here, of course. The hospital sent a car to pick up the nurses, doctors. They said they needed all the help possible. So she went. Told me to look out in case you came back home. And here you are." She says this in a voice completely devoid of enthusiasm. Good old Mak Siti.

My heart sinks. Mama isn't here. We've come all this way for nothing.

On impulse, I reach out a hand for Mak Siti's. Her skin feels like parchment, worn and wrinkled from years of hard work, but soft and yielding to the touch. "Thank you, Mak Siti," I say. "Thank you for looking out for me. I'm glad you're safe."

Her face softens. "It wasn't easy," she mutters. "So much yelling, so much noise. We all ran for Pak Samad's house—the big stone house, you know? We were worried they would set fire to our homes, so we packed ourselves in there like sardines to wait. Alang rounded up the other men, and they took all the weapons they could find and went to fight against those Chinese troublemakers from across the road." She shoots a quick glance at Vince, still standing a few paces away, then back at me. "That fat boy, Manaf, he acted so brave at first, shouting so loudly about how he was going to have Chinese heads on a platter. When the men left, he was as close to the front line as he could be, so eager to be a hero. When we came back out, after the fighting was over, we found him by Pak Samad's outhouse, white as a sheet. He fainted dead away when he saw them coming!" She cackles, shaking her head. I remember Manaf. He's a year or two older than me. When we were little, he liked to pull my hair and then run away, laughing; in recent years, this has given way to sitting with his friends on a special grassy knoll shaded by coconut trees and whistling to girls as they pass.

"Were . . . were there people who didn't make it back?" I ask, then immediately regret it. Of course there were people who didn't make it back.

Mak Siti shrugs, and I wonder how she can be so calm. Then I remember that she lived through the Japanese occupation too, her skin tough and hardened out of sheer necessity. "That's what happens," she says. "At least they took out more than a few of those terrible Chinese people. Now, would you like something to drink? Some tea?"

Before I can answer, a deep voice cuts through our chatter.

"Where is Safiyah?"

Through the trees strides Pakcik Adnan, Saf's father, as rigidly erect in posture and precise in step as he is when he makes his rounds at school. In fact, he looks much the same as always, except that his trousers, which usually sport creases so sharp they look like they could slice your fingertips off, are crumpled and unironed. If you've known him for most of your life, as I have, this is a sign of great inner turmoil.

"Where is Safiyah?" he asks me again, his glance never wavering from my face. His voice, clear and strong, seems to ring through the village, and pulls gazes toward us. A small crowd begins to gather.

I can feel a bead of sweat meander slowly down the side of my face. *Tell him, tell him, tell him*, the Djinn crows. *Tell him about your failure. Tell him how you let her die.* "We . . . we were at the movies, sir," I begin. Pakcik Adnan's eyes narrow. I feel an urge to tap so great that I almost keel over. *Not now, not now.* I forge on.

"We went to see the new Paul Newman movie. She was really excited about it. She wanted to watch it again as soon as it was over, because she said you wouldn't be home until late. . . ." My voice trails off as I wonder if I should be betraying Saf like this. But her father is staring at me, and I can't stop now, though I'd give anything to do just that.

"The lights went out in the theater. . . ." I swallow hard, finding it difficult to breathe. "These men came. Chinese men." A ripple goes through the watching crowd. "They forced Malays on one side and everyone else on the other. They let the non-Malays go."

"And the Malays?" Pakcik Adnan asks urgently. "What happened to the Malays? What happened to Safiyah?"

I can't bring myself to answer. I can't even bring myself to look at him. I stare at the ground, scratching patterns in the dirt with the tip of my shoe, tracing the number three over and over again, my face wet with tears I hadn't realized had begun to fall down my cheeks. "The men, the gangsters . . . they had weapons," I say quietly. "Pipes, sticks, knives." *Please understand what I'm trying to tell you*, I think. *Please don't make me go on.*

The silence that greets this pronouncement is so prolonged and so deafening that I can only stand it for so long before I look up.

Saf's father still stands before me, still holding himself straight and tall. But tears are streaming down his face, falling onto his pristine shirtfront, soaking the white cloth through. I have never seen him like this, and I can't bear to think my words are what caused it. I take a step toward him, wanting to offer some kind of comfort. "I miss her all the time. Every minute. I wish we were still together like always." It's only after I say the words aloud that I realize how true this is. I've been so preoccupied with keeping my mother safe that I've barely been able to mourn my best friend, and now I stagger slightly beneath the weight of my own grief.

Something changes then—something shifts inside him; I see it in his eyes, like a shutter has just been pulled down. He stares at me.

"How did you make it out?" His voice is a little ragged with grief, but he stands as tall and dignified as ever.

I feel it again, then, that small shift rifling through the crowd surrounding us, like leaves on a breeze.

"Someone saved me," I say.

"And that someone couldn't save Safiyah, too?"

I think back to Auntie Bee and what she did for me. "No," I say simply. "Not that way."

"So you left her to die." The words hit me like bullets, tearing through my conscience. The Djinn throws back his head and cackles.

"I . . . I . . . no, that's not . . . I had no choice!"

"You left her. That was a choice." *Didn't you?* the Djinn whispers. Guilt begins to ooze freely out of the wounds. I feel like I've been punched in the chest; all the wind has left me, and I fight to catch my breath. Did I have a choice? Had I been supposed to protect Saf the whole time? But all those visions . . . Mama is the one who will die if I don't obey. Right? *You'll never know now, will you? Because Saf is dead. You had the power to save her, and now she's dead.* For a moment, I can hear nothing but his cackles ringing in my ears.

"I never wanted this to happen," I choke out, tears already beginning to trickle down my cheeks.

"But it did," Pakcik Adnan says evenly. "And then for you to dare to come here, the place where you grew up, where so many suffer now because of the actions of those bloody hooligans, with one of *them*." He spits in Vince's direction, and Vince takes a step back, his face impassive, his arms crossed over his chest.

Pakcik Adnan turns his attention back to me, and I feel myself cowering in the face of his overpowering anger and sorrow. "You are a disgrace, Melati Ahmad," he says, his voice ringing in the deep silence. "You betray us with your associations, gallivanting about with Chinese pigs while your friends and family bleed at their feet. I wish my daughter never knew you." Then he spits again, this time at my feet, before turning his back and walking, with perfectly precise, measured steps, through the onlookers and back toward his home, where his wife stands waiting for him at the door.

"Are you okay?"

The onlookers have dispersed, and we are alone in the middle of Kampung Baru. I can't answer. I'm trapped in a web of numbers—the number of windows on all the houses surrounding us, the number of coconuts on those trees, the number of white pebbles on the ground, but only the white ones, not the others, the number of planks that make up the wooden fence of that house over there, anything but the recurring image of Saf being bludgeoned to death in the Rex, and the overwhelming feeling that I didn't do a damn thing to stop it. *Keep counting, Melati, keep counting.*

"We have to get out of here, Mel," Vince is saying, his voice low and urgent. "These villagers haven't exactly given me the warmest welcome, and I don't think the farewell is going to be any better. We have to go. Now."

He grabs me by the wrist and drags me along unprotesting as he walks quickly back to where we left the car, keeping a watchful eye on our surroundings. I stumble along behind him, not really taking it all in, still counting as I go. A traitor. Does trusting Vince make me a traitor? How do I know I can really trust him at all? *You can't,* the Djinn says, smiling winningly. *You shouldn't.*

A quick escape, as it turns out, isn't going to be possible. Jay's car is a wreck. It looks like what happens to paper when you've crumpled it into a little ball and then try to smooth it out again, covered with large dents and scratches all over. Every window has been smashed, and broken glass is everywhere; it crunches under the soles of Vince's brown leather shoes as he moves closer to survey the damage. Jay himself is nowhere to be seen.

"Stay back," he tells me. "I need to make sure it's safe." My mind immediately leaps into overdrive: a bomb explodes, blasting both the car and Vince's body into shreds; a man leaps out of the back seat, slicing Vincent's head off in one blow. Before I even realize what's happening, my shaking fingers are tapping furiously against my thighs.

"There's no way we can drive this thing," Vince says, emerging from the driver's seat, checking his palms carefully for any slivers of broken glass. "We're going to have to figure out another way to get home."

"Where's Jay?" I force myself to speak, my tongue thick and furry in my mouth.

"I don't know," Vince says, his brow creased with worry and frustration.

The numbers are failing. I'm meant to be keeping everyone safe, but everything is going wrong, and the numbers are failing. The world suddenly begins to tilt and sway, and I close my eyes to ward off the sensation of trying to walk on jelly, but all I see in the darkness is death. *You're failing, Melati*, the Djinn whispers. *You'll fail them all. Just like you failed Saf.*

I need to sit down.

It's only when I sink down to the ground, resting my aching head on my knees, that I see it, half-hidden among the wild, untamed grass along the clearing's edge: A crumpled blue square of cloth, with JS embroidered in the corner in navy blue thread, speckled with fresh blood.

CHAPTER TEN

I DON'T KNOW HOW LONG I sit there, clutching the handkerchief and trying to breathe. Vince says something to me; I can't figure out what it is over the roaring in my ears, so I just nod and hope he'll leave me alone, and he disappears. I know I should panic about this, but I'm too busy panicking about everything else to care. In his absence, the Djinn amuses himself by conjuring up imaginative ways for Jay to die and parading them through my head, in glorious technicolor. *Come on*, he says tauntingly, *you know what to do*. So I sit, counting each individual leaf on the coconut fronds overhead as they wave lightly in the breeze, weaving Jay's handkerchief clumsily in and out of my shaking fingers, hating the Djinn and hating myself.

In the distance, the rumble of a motorcycle getting closer and closer knocks me out of my stupor. *Bugger*, I think desperately, jumping to my feet and running to crouch low behind the car. When I look down, I realize my fingers are shaking. *Time to die*, the Djinn sings gleefully.

The motorcycle stops right in front of the car and someone cuts the engine. From my vantage point, I can hear the crunch of gravel as the rider disembarks.

Protect yourself, I think, *you need to protect yourself.*

A waste of time, the Djinn snorts.

Shut up, you.

Just beside me, a large rock lies half-buried in the dirt, and I quickly reach over and begin to work it out with my fingers. *Come on, come on.* The footsteps are coming closer, turning the corner, I almost have the rock free, come on, come on. . . . I swing around, my arm raised, ready to bash the guy's face in with my rock.

"Mel?"

It's Vince, staring at me with a bewildered expression on his face.

I lower my arm, feeling a little foolish. "I was just . . ." I gesture to the rock, then shrug and let it fall to the ground with a *thud*. "Umm. Where'd you get that?" I say, pointing to the motorcycle behind us. It's one the boys in the neighborhood would refer to as a motor kapcai, and from the way it shines in the evening sun, from the gleaming red and white of its hard plastic exterior all the way to the carefully polished black of its leather seat, it's obviously the pride and joy of its owner.

He looks down, suddenly bashful. "I, uh, I kind of . . . stole it."

Its owner, who, apparently, doesn't realize it's missing.

"You did?" I just stand there, looking at him. My mouth is hanging open a little, and I'm aware that I look like a fool. But this is inconceivable. I may only have known Vince for a few days, but he has such set ideas of right and wrong that it actually shocks me to know he's capable of outright theft.

"More like borrowing lah, really."

"Vince." I stare at him, and he sighs.

"I know, I know. But it was an emergency. I'm going to bring it back as soon as we're done." He reaches out and tugs at my sleeve. "Come on, I'm getting you home."

"You didn't happen to steal any helmets, did you?" I can't help teasing him a little as we sling ourselves on.

"I'll drive really carefully," he tells me seriously.

It won't help, the Djinn says quietly. As Vince guns the engine, I reach around with one arm to grab his waist, blushing in spite of myself. I am close enough to feel the heat emanating from him, close enough to breathe him in. One part of me carefully catalogs every minute detail of this: the way his hair curls up where it meets his shirt collar, the scent of him—fresh and clean, a mix of newly cut grass and lemony soap—the curve where his neck meets his shoulders. The other part of me pictures all the ways in which both of us will die on this journey.

With my other arm, I tap and tap and tap, counting in threes until the Djinn is satisfied.

We've been zooming along the near-empty roads for about fifteen minutes, past the leftover debris, the occasional body, the smoking husks of burning buildings, when I feel it: a movement, as if something is zipping past my right ear. As I turn my head to see what it is, I feel it again, just above my head this time. What is that?

One glance behind me reveals the answer: a group of guards, lounging against a car parked on the side of the street, one with his gun aimed right at us, casually sending shots ripping through the air toward us as if we're nothing more than target practice.

I turn back to Vince. "They're shooting at us!" I yell at him over the noise of the motorbike.

"What?!" He leans forward, driving even faster, and I hang on tight so I don't get thrown off. The wind snatches the band from my hair so that it whips wildly into my face and his. The bike careens left and right as he tries to avoid the shots.

Eventually, he drives into an alleyway and brings the bike to a sputtering halt. "What is it? Why are we stopping?" I ask, desperate to put as much distance between us and our attackers as we can.

Then I notice it: One of the bullets has ripped through the flesh on his left arm, just below his shoulder. The blood flows freely, staining his pale blue shirt in splotches of bright crimson.

No.

No, no, no, no, no.

Yes, the Djinn says, baring his teeth in wicked glee.

I grab for Jay's handkerchief into my pocket, folding it lengthwise with trembling hands. As I tie it tightly over the wound, the Djinn forces me to count a protective mantra in my head, tapping it in secret spots to make it safe as I can. Beads of sweat stand on Vince's head, and he's pale, but he doesn't complain.

"Just need to catch my breath," he says, smiling wanly at me as I force him to sit, his back against the wall.

"Okay," I say, and we sit in silence for a while.

Then, suddenly, we both sit up straight.

"Did you hear that?" I ask him. He nods. "Shush."

We're both perfectly still, waiting, listening. Then it comes again: a low, soft moan.

"Someone's hurt," he says, immediately struggling to his feet. I leap up to help him, and we both edge slowly along the alley, looking left and right for more guards.

When it comes again, the moan is louder, intense and soaked with pain. "There it is again!"

I point to a nearby shophouse. "It's coming from over there."

As we make our way toward it, I scour its façade for clues to what we might find inside. It doesn't yield much: The sign above it, once a bright blue now faded with time and the elements, is painted with Chinese characters in white; below them, a line proclaims TEA SHOP. One window is smashed, and the metal shutter that covers the doors has been forced open a crack, though I can't see anything beyond it other than darkness.

Vince goes first, pushing the shutters back farther to let us in, wincing at the pressure on his arm before cautiously stepping through. I follow him inside and immediately am engulfed in the musty scent of tea. On either side of us, floor-to-ceiling shelves are lined with jar after jar of leaves, each with labels I can't quite make out in the light that filters in weakly from the windows.

"Hello?" Vince calls out. "Hello, anyone there?"

At first, there is just silence. Then, from inside, we hear it: a groan.

"It's all right," he says, walking in a little farther. "It's all right. We're here to help you. Are you hurt?"

Then we see her, hunkering down behind the counter: a young woman, alone and very, very pregnant.

We shoot glances at each other and hurry to kneel beside her. "Hello," I say gently, laying a hand on her shoulder. She flinches at my touch, and looks at me warily. "It's okay," I tell her. "We just want to help you. You sound hurt. Are you?"

I can tell she's trying to decide if she can trust us. Her eyes dart back and forth, first to Vince, then to me, then to Vince again. But before she can speak, another wave of pain hits and she squeezes her eyes shut, biting her lips to suppress a groan. Her hands spasm protectively over her belly.

"Ma'am," Vince says softly, "ma'am, if you're in pain, we should get you to a hospital."

The woman's eyes fly open, and she shakes her head, her mouth set in a thin, obstinate line. "They'll hurt me," she whispers. "They'll hurt my baby. I saw them, shouting and hitting and burning things. I won't let them hurt my baby." She curls herself up as best she can, stroking her belly, her eyes squeezed shut.

I look at Vince despairingly. "How are we going to get her out of here?" I whisper. "We can't bring her on a motorcycle! And you're hurt, too." He waves away the last comment as if it doesn't matter. I can see his mind turning over possible solutions, but when he finally opens his mouth to speak, I can tell he's arrived at a conclusion he doesn't like.

"We'll have to ask them for help," he says.

"Them?"

"Them." He jerks his head toward the outside, and I suddenly realize who he means.

"*Them?* You mean the jerks who tried to shoot us?!"

He shrugs. "They're guards," he says. "Their job, first and foremost, is to protect citizens."

"That was your idea of them PROTECTING us?"

"If I just went and explained to them—"

"Explain?!" All I seem able to do is throw Vince's words back at him, just at a higher pitch and with a lot more hysterical disbelief behind them. "What if you don't get the chance to explain?! What if they kill you first?"

They will, the Djinn whispers, and I tap quickly against my thigh to shut him up.

"You have a better idea?" he asks me.

Of course I don't.

"I'll show them my Red Cross badge," he tells me. "They won't shoot me. They'll know I'm trying to help. They probably didn't see it when we were riding past." I can't tell if he's trying to convince me or himself.

"Sure," I say. Because what else can I do?

I kneel down again, beside the panting woman on the floor. "My name's Melati," I tell her, looking her right in the eye. "This is Vincent. What's your name?"

She exhales slowly. "Azizah," she says, trying to keep her voice steady. "My name is Azizah. My friends call me Jee."

"Okay, Jee," I say, "Vince is going out to get help, and I'll stay right here with you."

She nods, her eyes never leaving my face. Vince turns

to go. "I'll be right back," he says over his shoulder. *Sure you will*, the Djinn sneers, and reaches up to grip my heart with his cold, bony fingers.

"Will he really come back?" Jee whispers in his wake.

"Of course he will." I reach for her hand and grasp it, trying to reassure her with my touch.

She shuts her eyes. "But he's Chinese," she says. "Can we really trust him?"

"I do," I tell her. "I trust him completely."

She subsides, leaning back against the counter and groaning as another wave of pain hits her. But the Djinn doesn't. *You trust him, do you?* he says, grinning, his fingers still prodding and poking away at my heart, sending a stab of fear through it with each touch. *What's to stop him from going away and never coming back? What's to stop him from saving his own skin? Or else, what's to stop the soldiers from shooting him straight through the head, blasting it right off his body?*

I shudder.

Best start counting, the Djinn says, tossing my heart lightly up into my throat so that it's hard to breathe. And so I lift my bowed head, scan the shelves, and begin. *One, two, three, one, two, three, one, two, three . . .*

Before long, he returns, and I feel my heart wriggling itself out of the Djinn's grasp and blossoming with joy and relief.

But Vince's face, I notice, is anything but joyful.

"I can't get them to come," he says, flushed and agitated. "They won't follow me."

The woman whimpers, clutching her belly. She's trying her best to keep calm, not to complain, but her hands are clenched in white-knuckled fists, and beads of sweat are forming on her forehead.

I try to ignore the Djinn's yowl of glee and grab Vince by the elbow, leading him away and out of earshot. "Didn't you tell them it was an emergency?" I keep my voice low, so as not to worry Jee. But I don't think she can hear us over her own grunts and moans. I don't think she even sees us, she's in so much pain.

"I did, Mel," he says. "They wouldn't come."

"Why not?"

"They must have their reasons."

"Bloody hell, Vincent, she needs to get to the hospital, and we can't take her there on a motorcycle! Why didn't you—"

"Mel," Vince interrupts, rubbing his forehead with one hand. "They wouldn't come no matter what I told them. Because . . . well. Because I am who I am."

It's only then that it dawns on me.

"Because you're Chinese." I say it flatly, without emotion. Because of course that's why they won't come. A woman and her unborn child could die at my feet right now because some Malay soldiers won't pay any attention to a cry for help from a Chinese man. Inside me, the Djinn smiles delightedly, baring his sharp little teeth. *Look at all the death you bring with you.*

Vince is looking at me. "Di mana bumi dipijak . . . ," he says slowly.

"Huh?"

"We have to hold up their sky, Mel. Play by their rules."

I stare at him, openmouthed. "Are you serious? These are the guys who tried to shoot us!"

"Because they thought we were both Chinese. But you aren't. You're Malay; you're one of them."

"I am NOT one of them!"

"As far as they know, you are. They'll help you. They'll help you get her to the hospital."

I shake my head. "No. They'll never let you come with me. We'll be separated."

"I'll follow on the bike. I'll meet you there."

My eyes are filling with tears, and I blink them back angrily. Being apart means I won't be able to keep him safe. Being apart means never knowing what dangers could befall him.

Being apart means being alone.

The woman groans, biting her bottom lip so hard that she draws blood. My fingers spasm against my thighs, begging to tap out these anxieties, one by one.

"I'm not sure I can do this," I whisper. "They'll die, and this time you won't be able to say it isn't my fault, because it will be, one hundred percent, my fault."

Vince exhales noisily, and I can sense his frustration. I can even understand it. I'm frustrated with me too. "Everybody dies, Mel," he says. "The only real question is when. The truth is that she may die if we stay here and do nothing, or she may live. She may die on the way to the hospital, if we find a way to get her there—or she may live. She may make it to the hospital and die anyway. Or she may live. It's a game of chance, or destiny, or God's plan—whichever you believe." He glances at the woman as she pants, trying hard to control her pain. "At least if we try to get her to the hospital, we know she'll be with people who know what they're doing. If we're her only chance of making it there, why not tip those odds a little more in her favor?"

You're going to get them all killed, that familiar rasping voice says, and suddenly, I am filled with white-hot rage. I am tired of being the Djinn's plaything. I am tired of the constant tapping and counting, tired of my brain never stopping, never staying still.

Shut up, I think. *You're not me. You don't know what I can or can't do. You don't get to decide.*

I look at Vincent and nod. "Okay," I say. "Let's do it."

Deep breath, Melati. Let's go.

• • •

The guards are standing around a car just a little way down the road when I emerge from our hiding place, smoking and chatting like it's Sunday morning at the neighborhood kopitiam. The scent of cigarette smoke wafts over to where I stand, bathed in sweat and trying to suppress the urge to run as fast as I can in the opposite direction.

"Assalamualaikum!" I try to greet them as loudly as I can, but the Djinn reaches up to my throat and squeezes so nothing comes up but a cracked whisper.

Damn it.

I clear my throat and try again. "Assalamualaikum!"

You know the plan, Melati. Just follow the plan. The Muslim greeting will identify you immediately as being as Not Chinese as they come, so they'll want to help you. Plus—and this is pretty important—it'll make them maybe not want to shoot you on sight. Which is a bonus.

Trust my stupid broken brain to bring up their guns at a time like this. My head is throbbing and my teeth itch and I'm aching to count something, anything. Quickly, I tap my right index finger on my left wrist—Vince says I have to keep my hands visible so they don't think I'm concealing any weapons.

Again, Melati.

"Assalamualaikum!" I'm practically roaring it down the streets at this point, and it is a relief when one of the guards finally turns toward me, frowning as he tries to locate the source of the commotion.

Showtime.

"Tolong! Help!" I yell, waving my arms as I jog toward them. "Help me! Please!"

Now all four of them are looking at me, and one of them straightens up, dropping his cigarette and grinding it under his feet.

"What is it?" he growls, keeping his hand on the rifle slung over his shoulder. "Little girls shouldn't be out and about at a time like this."

"Especially not when they're disturbing the peace," drawls another, before taking a drag of his cigarette. I can feel his eyes traveling up and down my body, lingering insolently in select spots, and feel the bile rise to my throat.

Now I'm more pissed off than ever.

"I'm sixteen, thank you," I say, setting my chin and addressing my remarks entirely to the first soldier. "And I came to you because I need help. That *is* what you're supposed to do, isn't it? Help the people?"

The first soldier grunts in response, and I take that as a sign to continue. "There's a woman in that building over there, and she's pregnant, and I think she's about to give birth," I say. "She's in a lot of pain. She needs to get to a hospital." My eyes keep flitting over to their guns, and I can't help wondering which one launched the bullet that tore a bloody path through Vincent's arm. *Focus, Melati.*

"Sounds like a real problem," the second soldier says. He hasn't stopped staring at me. "What do we get in return for helping you?" His tone is perfectly pleasant, his grin wide and leering. I want to take the knife from his holster and slash it from his face.

"Shut up, Rahman." The first one is clearly the one in charge here, and Rahman subsides with a scowl.

The soldier looks at me. "There's a car we can use here," he says, gesturing to the black sedan behind them. "Can your friend walk? Or does she need help with that?"

Relief floods through me. "I think she could use some help," I say. "She's just over there, inside that shophouse— that one, just there."

He nods. "All right. Arif, start the car and bring it around. You two, stay here and keep watch. I expect a full report of any incidents when we get back."

The others nod, and the soldier and I—"You can call me Mat," he tells me—make our way toward the shop- house. Vincent is nowhere to be seen. In the middle of the room, right where I left her, Jee is panting harder now, her face completely pale, her jaw set, her eyes closed. I kneel down beside her. "Time to go, Jee," I say gently. "We have to get to the hospital now."

I might as well be talking to stone.

"Jee?" I say again, touching her shoulder. "Jee?"

Great. I just risked my life for a woman who appears to be set on giving birth in the middle of an abandoned shophouse.

Then, the strangest thing happens. Mat, who has thus far been hanging back, just watching us, decides to come forward and kneel on Jee's other side.

This is going to be great.

"Hello, Jee," he says.

No answer. The only sound that fills the room is Jee's shallow panting. I can't help myself; I start counting them, finding a small comfort in the familiar rhythm: one, two, three, one, two, three, one, two, three . . .

"Jee, we have to get you to the hospital now, okay?" Mat says, keeping his voice low, gentle.

Still no response.

"I know what you must be feeling," he continues. "Well, not know, obviously, because how can I? But when my wife was having our son, she was just like you. She wanted to concentrate, and I just kept bugging her—asking her all sorts of stupid questions, making all sorts of stupid comments. 'Are you okay? Does it hurt? Is he coming now?' She told me afterward that she never wanted to punch me in the face so much."

Jee has her eyes open now and is looking at him with a slightly dazed expression. The pants have given way to periodic grunts and groans.

"I know you've got this covered," Mat says gently. "I know you're worried about setting foot out there, with everything that's going on."

"What if someone tries to hurt the baby?" Her voice is barely a croak.

"They'd have to get through me first," he says. He means it, I think. He really means it.

I guess she thinks so too. "Okay," she breathes. "Okay."

Five minutes later, we're all sitting in the car, and Arif is driving toward the hospital as though he's being chased by monsters. In the back seat, Jee grips my hand so hard it goes numb; the upside is that it keeps me from tapping.

I know we're in the middle of an intense situation here, but part of my mind—the part that's still sane—is busy doing victory laps and turning cartwheels. I did it! I went up to strangers—*armed* strangers!—because someone else needed help, and I succeeded. I didn't let my stupid broken brain get in the way. I didn't rely on someone else to save me. And I didn't give in to the numbers, not even once! For the first time in a long, long time, I'm beginning to feel like normal is within reach after all. I can do anything. I can save others. I can save myself. And I can find Mama.

"We're here." Arif's voice puts a screeching halt to my euphoria. I look up and realize we're at the main entrance of the Kuala Lumpur General Hospital. Mama's hospital.

Mama is here! My brain is screaming for me to run as

fast as I can, dash inside, look for Mama, make sure she's safe. But I stop myself. Jee first. Mat wrenches open the car door, and between us we haul Jee into the emergency room, where she's immediately swallowed up by a frenzied group of nurses and attendants, leaving us standing uncertainly in the lobby, side by side under the bright red letters spelling out EMERGENCY. There are nine letters; three times three. It's a good sign, I decide.

"Thank you," I say, looking up at Mat. He rubs his nose, suddenly bashful. "Just part of the job," he mutters. Then he pulls himself together. "Will you be all right?"

I nod. "My mother is here," I say. I can feel the relief unfurl inside me, blooming like fresh flowers.

"Okay, then. Take care, young lady," he says, striding off, presumably to find Arif and get back to work.

It's only when they're both gone that I really stop to take stock of my surroundings.

The hospital is chaos. Nurses and doctors run to and fro, wheeling complicated machines, carrying stacks of charts. At the registration counter, an attendant wearing a harassed expression is patiently trying to help an increasingly hysterical older woman. "But where is she?" she keeps asking. "Why can't you tell me where she is? How will I know if she's hurt?" "We're doing everything we can to find out, madam," the attendant says, straining to keep her voice even, polite. On the benches and chairs, dozens wait their turn in silence. One boy, no older than ten, whimpers in the corner; his mother murmurs soothingly in his ear. There's no way to tell the original color of the blood-soaked towel she's pressing to his face. "Ricochet," I hear one nurse mutter to another as they flip through a chart. "The bullet pinged off a wall and ripped through his cheek." Along one corridor, bags are piled high on gurneys. "You can't leave these here!" I hear one doctor yell at the beleaguered attendant, who shrugs. "There's no room left in the morgue," he says. "I've got nowhere else to put them."

My euphoria has disappeared, in its place that familiar, dark dread, that feeling of wanting to burst out of my own skin. I have come to the house of death, and I'm completely unprepared for its assault on my senses. My mind moves at the speed of light. Here's Mama, riddled with bullets; here's Mama, her skull crushed by the beating of a heavy truncheon; here's Mama, throat slit from ear to ear.

I start pacing, and as I walk, I count—a barrier, a protective incantation to ward off the specter of death. I count every step I take, every word and every letter on every sign. I count the number of chairs in the waiting room, the number of people on the chairs. I assign them to groups and count them off—men versus women, adults versus children, long-haired women versus short-haired women, men with black hair versus men with gray hair. Nothing works.

My thoughts flutter like poisonous butterflies, from Mama to Saf to Vincent, from Jee's pale face to the leer on Rahman's, from Frankie's burning, righteous anger to the worried expressions of Uncle Chong and Auntie Bee. Death, death, death for them all, and it's all my fault.

But Mama's here, I remind myself, fighting to stay in control. Mama's here; Mak Siti said so. I'll find her, and once I see her I know everything will be okay again.

I just have to find her.

I run, as fast as I can, to the nurses' station, pounding through the familiar, brightly lit corridors. Left here, then right, then up the stairs, then I skid to a stop, almost slipping on the polished floor.

There it is before me, bathed in harsh fluorescent light, and buzzing with activity. Nurses slip in and out, consulting charts, talking on the phone, conferring with doctors and one another in hushed tones. I look anxiously around for a familiar face. Then I spot Auntie Fatimah, my mother's lunch buddy and confidante, and a regular visitor at our home. Relief floods through me. "Auntie Fati!" I call out, jogging toward her. "Auntie! Over here!"

She turns, squinting at me over the top of her glasses. "Melati?"

I fling myself into her arms. I don't think I've ever been so happy to see anyone before. She hugs me back before pulling away. "Are you all right?" She's scanning my body up and down, her expert eye clocking every scrape, every bump, every bruise. "Are you hurt? What's happened?"

"I'm okay, Auntie Fati," I say, smiling. "Honestly, I am. I'm looking for my mother. Have you seen her?"

She frowns again, her right hand reaching up to massage her neck as she considers the question. "I know I saw her . . . When was that?" she says, and my heart lifts crazily. "It's been such a blur, I can't really remember. I do recall being really happy when she walked through the door. We were just so swamped with everything, we really needed all the hands we could get. Still do. But we've been so busy since then. . . . I just don't know where she went. Hey, Anita"—she turns to another nurse seated at the counter scribbling on a chart. "Have you seen Salmah anywhere?"

Nurse Anita looks up from her notes. "Oh, no," she says. "Salmah was here that first day, but she left a couple of days ago. I heard her tell the head nurse she had to go home, make sure her daughter was okay."

"Well, there you go," Auntie Fati says, turning back to me. "I tell you, time has gone by so fast here with all the bodies coming in, I don't even know what day it is, if I'm standing on my head or on my feet. . . . Eh, Melati, are you all right?"

I can't speak. The Djinn is on a gleeful, nasty rampage: Ice courses through my veins, sending a thousand painful little pinpricks shooting throughout my entire body. His

CHAPTER ELEVEN

THE MOTORCYCLE JUDDERS TO A stop in front of
the house. My legs feel strangely wobbly, and Vince has to
help me off, wincing when I grab his arm to steady myself.
They bandaged it up pretty well at the hospital, but I can
tell he's still in pain. "Sorry," I whisper.

As we walk toward the house, a curtain flutters in the
breeze and the Djinn begins to swirl around in my stomach, trying to get my attention. *Something's wrong*, he
whispers, *don't you feel it? Something's wrong, Melati*. I
strain to keep my breathing even, keeping my eyes focused
on the house, but I can't shake the feeling that the Djinn is
right. What am I missing?

Then it hits me.

"Check the windows," Uncle Chong had commanded
on that first night. "Make sure they're secure." And they've
stayed tightly shut and locked ever since—I should know, I
checked them often enough in those fevered nights, trying

cold, bony hands close in around my throat, and I fall to my knees, dizzy and gasping for air, a million spots dancing in front of my eyes. I squeeze them shut, but behind my eyelids Mama's corpse lies cold and rigid on Petaling Street. My heart pounds a frantic, erratic beat, so hard that I'm actually afraid it will explode into a million tiny pieces. I want nothing more than to rip myself out of my own body, free myself from the Djinn's grasp and run as far and as fast as I can. *That's what you get for getting cocky*, he tells me. *That's what you get for thinking you could beat me. As if you could.* The spots in front of my eyes begin to merge together, millions and millions of them, until all I see around me is deep, inky black. And then a whisper from the darkness: *You'll never beat me, Melati.*

I don't know how long I stay this way on the floor, my arms locked across my chest, my head bowed, my eyes shut.

All I know is that when I open my eyes again, Vince is carrying me in his arms. I blink up at him sleepily. There is a bandage wrapped around his injured arm; the glow from the fluorescent lights forms a halo around his head.

"Come on, Melati," he says quietly. "Let's go home."

to make sure we all stayed safe. Yet there it is, the curtain swaying in the breeze.

Except for some jagged pieces along the edges, the glass from the window is gone.

I can feel my pulse quickening. Vince is ahead of me, his hand outstretched to open the door. I want to say something, to warn him, but the Djinn grabs hold of my tongue and stops me from speaking. All I can do is watch the frown on Vince's face as the door swings open at his touch, unlocked; the confusion quickly giving way to shock and pain as he takes in the scene before him; the flash of anger as he quickly strides inside.

I take a deep breath to steel myself, then head in after him.

Inside, I have to pick a path through the debris on the floor: overturned furniture, bits of broken glass from the windows, the remnants of Auntie Bee's delicate blue patterned plates and bowls. Vince is standing in the middle of it all, silent, unmoving but for his hands, which are balled into fists and shaking.

"It happened a couple of hours ago," a voice says, and we both turn to see Frankie leaning against the door frame, silhouetted in the dying rays of the evening sun. "A mob came. Started burning and looting the houses. Malay, of course," he says, nodding in my direction. "All while the guards stood back and let them. Must take care of your own, right?"

"What happened to Ma and Baba?" Vince's voice is strangled.

"Ba and I tried to fight them off, but some cibai Malay coward hit him on the head from behind, and when I went to help him they ran off," Frankie says. "He's okay. Bruised. Ma is really scared. I took them to Chin Woo Stadium; that's where they're letting people like us take shelter. You know, people the Malays have managed to take everything from."

"Frankie . . ." The two brothers look at each other, and I wonder if they're about to get into another fight. "Thanks for being here," Vincent says, and though his voice is still strained I can hear the thread of sincerity in it. "Thanks for taking care of them. While I was out there . . ."

Frankie shrugs. "No point talking about it now," he says. "I'm just here to get some clothes and stuff for them. Don't hang around here; it's dangerous." He walks past us toward the master bedroom. Soon, we hear muffled *thud*s and *bang*s as he rummages through the wardrobe and vanity.

I look over at Vince, his eyes closed, his hands clenched into tight fists by his side. "I'm sorry, Vincent," I say, because what else is there to say? But he doesn't answer, and eventually I slip quietly away and leave him to his thoughts.

· · ·

Sitting outside is probably the worst thing to do at a time like this, but I don't know where else to go, so I settle myself on an upturned ceramic plant pot just outside to wait. The sky is ablaze with streaks of orange, pink, purple, and the breeze carries the merest whiff of flowers—jasmine. For once, the Djinn is silent. It's so peaceful, so beautiful, that I could almost forget everything that has led us to this point.

A movement in the corner of my eye jolts me out of my reverie. It's Frankie, bearing a small, stuffed suitcase in each hand.

"I'm sorry about your parents, Frankie," I tell him. It's my third apology in thirty minutes, but I don't know what else I can say. "I'm glad they weren't badly hurt."

He regards me, his head tilted to one side. I search his expression, but can't tell what he's thinking. When he speaks, he speaks slowly, thoughtfully. "Even after my father was hit, even when we were trying to get him to a doctor, you know what he was saying? 'Aiya, don't blame them lah, they don't know any better, poor things.' He was still trying to justify their actions, still trying to be under-standing and forgiving."

I can feel tears welling in my eyes. Frankie goes on, his eyes never leaving my face.

"My parents were never anything but nice and good to anyone—Chinese, Malay, Indian, whoever. But the Malays didn't care. They looked at them and saw outsiders, not worthy of their time or mercy. What's the use of being good if it just gets you trampled on?"

I can feel my body burn hot with shame, frustration, anger. I can't make myself meet his gaze. Are we all as bad as he says? *Yes*, says that voice in my ear. *Yes, you are. What makes you think you can protect anyone? You failed Saf, you failed Mama, and now you've failed Auntie Bee and Uncle Chong, too.*

After a pause, he turns toward the car. "Tell Vincent I'm going back to Chin Woo," he says over his shoulder as he walks away. Before long, I hear the sound of the Standard puttering down the road.

I sit outside until the last of the evening light deepens into night. I hear mosquitoes buzz lazily past my ears, but I don't even flinch. I'm too busy counting jasmine blossoms through eyes blurry with tears.

Eventually, Vince comes outside. I look up at him from my spot on the ground. "Come on," he says, brushing past me. "Let's go." He looks more tired than I've ever seen him.

"I . . . in a minute," I say, my fingers moving feverishly in my pockets. 249, 252, 255 . . . Wait, did I count that right? Is it 255 or 256? 257? I freeze, paralyzed by my own doubt. *You've messed it up now*, the Djinn growls. *Do it again. You have to do it again, or it won't be right, and your mother dies, and Vince dies, and his parents die. Everyone dies, because of you.*

My stomach is churning, and my chest is tight. Every breath is a struggle.

"Come on, Melati," Vince says impatiently. "I need to make sure my parents are okay."

So do I, I want to yell at him, but I can't, yelling is just another distraction, and I can't afford to be distracted now, or else I'll have to start all over again.

"MELATI." Vince's voice is like a gunshot in the quiet of the garden. "My parents have been hurt, and you're keeping me from seeing them! What's wrong with you?"

"I . . . just wait a second," I choke out. I'm flushed and my face is streaked with tears, but I can't answer, I can't, I can't lose my place again. I can't let them all die. "I have to keep counting. I have to finish."

Vince clicks his tongue in frustration. When he speaks again, his tone is as cold and sharp as a diamond's edge. "You and your numbers," he says bitterly. "I wish I'd never met you and never heard about your stupid numbers. I could have been home. I could have been here to help Frankie; I could have kept my parents safe. And now, when I could be there with them, we're stuck in here because you're too busy counting to get your butt moving. God, you're a piece of work, Melati. You're so bloody selfish, you know that?"

And with that, he turns and heads back to the motorcycle to wait for me.

I want to follow him, to apologize, to explain, to make things right. But I can't move from my spot. Instead, I count and count until I reach a number that feels safe—a perfect three hundred—hating myself more and more with each passing second.

In the distance, I see it: Chin Woo Stadium, looming over a concrete parking lot, the streetlights glinting off the windows that cover the entire façade of the circular building. Over the main entrance, large red Chinese characters stand proudly. "What does Chin Woo mean?" I ask after Vince has parked the bike and cut the engine. It's the first thing either of us has said since our showdown in the garden, and I'm not really sure if he'll answer me. But I'm low and hurting and desperate for some kind of normalcy.

In the time he takes to respond, Mama, Auntie Bee and Vince himself die, one at a time, with varying degrees of gore. I flinch with each one as if I'm taking blows, tapping the panic away furiously, my fingers hidden in my pockets. "The essence of martial arts," he says finally. "The association that runs it does a lot of activities here, including swimming and wushu. We used to come here to swim, once in a while."

He doesn't look at me when he tells me all of this. He hasn't really looked at me since we left the house.

"Come on," he says. "Let's go look for my parents."

Inside, the great hall is packed with families seeking refuge from the chaos going on outside. In one corner, a mother dozes off while breastfeeding a squirming baby; he moves here and there, restless, exposing her nipple, but she doesn't even notice. I look away, embarrassed. A pair of little girls shriek as they dash past, weaving and ducking through the crowd, leaving a trail of giggles and messes in their wake. An old woman spoons porridge into her husband's mouth as he sits propped against the wall, one arm in a sling. Off to the left, a small group has commandeered a couple of tables and are sorting through what seems to be a massive amount of food supplies. "Another delivery from the markets and sundry shops," I hear a woman saying. "We need to get these repacked and start sending them out."

Vincent, who has been scanning the room anxiously, suddenly straightens up. "There they are," he says, and begins to work his way through the crowd. I hang back, inexplicably nervous. *Why should they want to see you? Why should any of these people want to see you?*

What do you mean? I've been trying not to engage with the Djinn, but I'm genuinely confused.

You failed them, he says, caressing the back of my neck with a cold hand, trailing goosepimples in his wake. *You took their food and their hospitality and all they got in return was hurt.*

I am suddenly acutely aware of the beads of sweat standing on my forehead, the fact that my hands are convulsively clenching and unclenching themselves. I read a book once about how our bodies are primed to protect us; faced with times of extreme danger or stress, we either choose to go into battle or run for safety. Fight or flight, they call it. And right now every nerve ending in my body is screaming at me to run, run as fast and as far away as I can—well, almost. There is one corner of my mind where a light seems to pulse, away from the Djinn's endless taunts, one corner where a voice that sounds a lot like mine whispers: *You could fight. You could fight him, Melati, you could fight your Djinn. And you could win.*

I wish it were easier to hear. I wish it were easier to believe.

"Melati!" Auntie Bee charges through the crowd toward me and wraps me up in a huge hug, almost suffocating me.

"Hi, Auntie Bee," I manage to croak out. The Djinn casts a spotlight on all her worst injuries—the cut above her eye, the bruise spreading across her left cheek, the slight limp when she walks—and snickers. *Look what you did.*

"Aiyo, I was so worried about you all! We waited so long for you two to come back, I kept thinking about what was happening to you both. You know lah, you hear all these stories . . ." She shudders delicately. "But never mind, never mind, we don't talk about that. Are you all right? Are you hurt?" She holds me at arm's length, looking me up and down.

"I'm fine, Auntie Bee," I say. "Vincent kept me safe."

Just like you were supposed to keep them safe.

I shake my head again, hard, fast. Auntie Bee is still talking. "Your poor uncle, his head hurts a little bit but it's fine lah really, I think he just wants people to make a fuss. I told him, he's so hardheaded it wouldn't make any difference. . . ."

I wonder how your mother is doing, the Djinn muses, waving his arms so that my stomach turns and churns, making me queasy.

". . . of course, he thought he could fight them off, and I told him, you see lah, you see! See what happens when you try to be a hero! He thinks he's still a young man, your uncle, but well, clearly . . ."

I wonder if she'll suffer, when it happens. If there'll be much pain.

I can't do this. I can't. My mind flails around for something to fixate on and seizes on the tiled floor: thousands upon thousands of scuffed pale green tiles stretching out all across the hall.

". . . Pity about the house, ah girl, but of course, better it than us, right? Oh well, we will stay here for a while, then maybe find someplace else. It isn't too bad here, really. . . ."

The little squares arrange and rearrange themselves

into patterns only I can see; I count each and every one, over and over again, breathing as deeply as I can. The words, when they come, clang in place in my head one by one, heavy as lead.

Do you think Saf was in pain when she died?

I recoil physically at this, sucking in a breath sharply, wriggling myself free of Auntie Bee's grasp. "Ah girl, are you okay?" I look at her kindly face staring at me, soft with sympathy, and suddenly I can't bear it.

"Just need some air, Auntie," I manage to say, smiling at her weakly before stumbling away. I have to get away.

As far away as I can.

Outside, I lean my head against the cool concrete surface of the building, my eyes shut, trying to get a grip on the thoughts that swirl and crash within. *Don't listen to him, Melati. Don't listen to the Djinn.* I try to keep my breathing as deep and even as I can, counting the beats as I inhale and exhale. *One, two, three. One, two, three. One, two, three. The girl with kaleidoscope eyes*, I think, or a waltz. The ones Mama listens to on Sunday mornings.

Used to listen to, the Djinn says. *Past tense.*

No, not you. "Go away," I say aloud.

"Sorry."

"What?" I open my eyes, startled, and see Vince standing before me, frowning.

"I didn't realize I was disturbing you."

"No! No, sorry. I was just . . ." I wave a hand around lamely, as if I can draw the words out of the air to explain myself. "I was just talking to myself, I guess."

He doesn't respond, and I don't want to make him. Instead, I lean back against the wall and wait. He walks over to stand beside me and sags against the wall himself, his head tilted back, his eyes shut.

When he eventually speaks, his voice is low, and I have to lean in to catch every word.

"They're all right."

I nod. "I know. I spoke to your mother for a bit."

He lets out a breath. "I'm going to take them away from here tonight."

He's avoiding my eyes, but I can fill in the blanks without him looking at me. "You're leaving?"

"I want to take them somewhere safe. Maybe to Kelantan—we've got some relatives there, and I hear it's pretty peaceful."

What about me? I want to ask him. *What happens to me now?* But the words stick in my throat. Instead I say, "I understand," and I do. Why wouldn't I, when all I ever think about is keeping my own mother safe?

He looks at me then. "They've taken the Malays over to Stadium Negara," he says. "I can take you there, if you like. That's where your mother is, probably. Everyone who lost a home or has nowhere else to go . . . that's where they ended up."

Mama. I can feel the tiny bubbles of relief floating up through my murky thoughts. "Thank you," I say.

"You're welcome."

He straightens up, brushes dirt off his dark trousers with two brisk strokes, and heads back inside, leaving me to contemplate the night sky.

In the silence, the Djinn stirs.

Told you he'd leave you.

I'm too tired to fight him off. Instead, I let him enfold me in a beguilingly soft, dark blanket of misery, and cry and cry and cry until my head is heavy and my throat is sore and my eyes swell so that the city lights blur and merge into a beautiful, chaotic mess.

The Standard has been through a lot in the past few days, and it takes a bit of work to get it up the gentle incline toward Stadium Negara. The stadium sits in all its stark, modern splendor upon its hill, its windows reflecting the dim streetlights around it.

Vince frowns as the car sputters and coughs along. "I hope this thing makes it to Kelantan in one piece," he mutters, frowning as he clutches the wheel. "Otherwise I'm going to have a hell of a time figuring out how to get us there."

A hell-of-a racing-story. A hell-of-a-romance. I'm swept away by a tidal wave of memories so intense that I gasp; it's like the Djinn has socked me in the stomach. One by one, I watch the pictures float by: Saf, throwing her head back to laugh her raucous laugh that her father always thought so terribly unladylike; Saf, bobbing her head in time to the beat of the latest Top 40 tune; Saf, giggling uncontrollably as she plotted and schemed to steal one of the hand-painted Paul Newman posters from the cinema.

All that time you spent worrying about your mother, the Djinn whispers, *and in the end it was Saf you gave up.*

My thoughts won't stop racing, but one keeps coming up again and again: Was it all a trick? Was it Saf I was meant to be protecting with my rituals all along? But what about Mama?

Why think about her at all? She'll be dead the minute you stop counting.

Shut up, I think. *Shut up, shut up, shut up.* I count the interlocking triangles decorating the stadium's façade in increasingly complicated groups and patterns, sweating slightly as I do it. It used to be that the numbers were what the Djinn demanded in return for keeping my mother alive; these days it seems they're the only way I can keep him quiet long enough to see straight, long enough to take back my thoughts and make them mine again.

Silly girl, the Djinn says. *Who says I'm ever going to*

leave you? You're mine. And he wraps his arms around me in a tender embrace.

No. No, no, no. I double down on the counting, tapping lightly, furiously on my knees, a symphony of beats to accompany the numbers. I can see Vince observing me out of the corner of his eye as he drives, but he doesn't say anything, so I ignore him.

I need to focus.

There's a tap on Vince's window as we roll up to the entrance. A uniformed police officer gestures for him to roll it down. "What's your business here?" he asks pleasantly.

"I have a pass, sir," Vincent says, handing over the slip of paper. "I'm just dropping her off." He nods in my direction. "She's looking for her mother, sir; they got separated when the troubles began."

"Malay?" he asks, glancing in my direction. Vince nods.

The officer glances at the paper, nods, and hands it back. "All right, then," he says. "Go ahead and drop her off, but you'd best be on your way. There are some who may not look too kindly on you in there."

"Thank you, sir."

I've been silent throughout this entire exchange, but only because I need to get this right. *Concentrate, Melati.*

Deftly, my fingers tap and stroke, weaving my safety net all over the car, all over Vincent. If I can't be with him, the least I can do is help protect him. *Again*, the Djinn says, wrapping cold fingers around the base of my spine. *That's not right. Again.* I go over it again and again, counting and tapping until everything feels just right. Then I sit back and exhale.

Just in time. Vince pulls up to the main entrance and kills the engine. The sudden silence seems loud, unnatural, stilted. It's like we haven't just spent the past week in each other's company.

"Well . . . ," he begins, then stops, unsure of what to say next.

"Thank you," I tell him. "Thank you for everything. You and your family, you all saved my life. I won't forget that." I can't look at him. I think if I do I may cry.

"Take care of yourself," he says.

"Good-bye," I say.

And then there really isn't much more to say. I open the door, slide off the cracked vinyl seat, and close it firmly. *No silly nonsense, Melati; it's better that you leave. You failed them. And you need to find Mama, so you won't fail her, too.*

I turn around and walk away without looking back, so that he doesn't have to see the tears when I finally let myself cry.

It's just you and me now, sayang, the Djinn purrs, reclining in the pit of my stomach, a look of smug satisfaction on his face.

When I finally push open the heavy double doors to the stadium, the first thing that hits me is just how much bigger it seems. Then I realize that it isn't that the stadium is that much bigger—it's that there are fewer people here. Unlike the packed walls of the Chin Woo Stadium, where people had to shrink themselves to fit somewhere between one another and their belongings besides, here families can move around more freely, taking up larger spaces to create some semblance of home for themselves. There is less tension in the air. There is room to breathe.

I head straight to the table in the corner where volunteers are presiding over food rations. "Excuse me," I say timidly to one of them, his armband marking him as a member of the Red Cross, like Vince. Even thinking his name sends a sharp pang shooting through my chest.

No, stop, Melati. Don't think about Vince, not now.

The man turns to look down at me, his expression impatient. "What is it?"

"I'm sorry to interrupt. I just got here. . . . I'm looking for my mother."

He rubs the back of his neck. "Impossible for me to tell you where one person is in all this mess," he says, gesturing to the hall. "No time to be flipping through lists and things. Why don't you wander around and take a look? Let me know if you can't find her and we'll try to help." Then he turns back to his work.

Okay. Let's take a look.

I begin wandering the hall, picking my way through the pockets of spaces marked by the refugees. There may be fewer people here than at Chin Woo, but they all bear the same scars: cuts, bruises, bandaged limbs, tearful faces, haunted looks. I pass one old man with snow-white hair and his right arm in a sling, sitting with his back against the wall and his eyes shut, reciting passages from the Quran from memory. The melodious lilt of his voice wafts along behind me as I make my way through the hall.

I recognize the lines; this is surah Yasin, what my mother often refers to as the heart of the Quran. Every time I hear it, it conjures up memories of my father's funeral and the house full of men and women swaying as they recited Yasin in unison around Abah's stiff body, wrapped tightly in white cloth and laid out on a mattress in the middle of the room. Every week since, I've heard my mother recite the surah every Thursday night, her voice low and sweet. She says it's in memory of Abah, and for her parents, the grandmother and grandfather who died before I was old enough to retain any memories of them. A dirge for the dead.

The word "dead" sets off a chain reaction of deaths in my head; the Djinn sets them up like rows of dominoes, and one by one I watch them fall, as if in slow motion: Abah, Saf, Jay, Auntie Bee, Uncle Chong, Vince, Mama. I grit my teeth and count each person as I pass, sorting them mentally into groups; first by gender, then by age, then by the colors they wear, then by wounded versus nonwounded. . . .

Then I stop. Wounded number twenty-one, a woman sitting with an ankle wrapped in gauze propped up on a wooden carton. Her white nurse's uniform is spotted with grime and, here and there, blood. That must be . . . surely that's . . .

"Auntie Tipah?"

The woman looks up, her hands still holding an open bottle and a cotton pad that she's been using to dab some small cuts and wounds along her legs, her brows still furrowed in concentration. It takes a minute or two for her to recognize me. The minute she does, her eyes widen. "Melati?"

That's her, all right; I'd recognize that raspy smoker's voice anywhere.

I go to kneel beside her and she envelops me in a warm but awkward hug, given the position she's in. "What are you doing here, my dear?" she asks me, gripping my elbow as though she's worried I'll run away. "Where's your mama? Is she all right? I've been wanting to see her, to thank her properly." Her eyes are bright, feverish.

My heart, so light just a minute earlier, turns to lead and *thud*s to my feet. "You mean . . . you mean she isn't here?"

A shadow falls across her face. She turns away from me and busies herself tidying the loose ends of the gauze that binds her ankle. "No, she isn't," she says.

"Do you know where she could be?" There is a tremble in my voice I can't quite mask.

Auntie Tipah sighs. "We left the hospital together that day," she says. "Your mother wanted to go and see if you made it home safe, and I wanted to be with my family. Everyone did; we were so worried. To see so many dead and wounded come in—they looked like they'd been in a war." She pauses to tuck a stray hair behind her ear; she still won't look at me. "So we started out on our bicycles. We were both scared, but we were trying not to show it. 'They won't hurt us,' she told me. 'We're no threat to anyone, you and I.' And she was right, you know, how could we be a threat to anyone? Your mother's just about fifty kilos, if that, and look at my skinny little arms!" She pauses to flex a barely noticeable muscle. "See? Some threat." She sniffs and lets her hands fall to her lap.

"I didn't notice the stone in the road," she says, lacing her fingers together, then apart, together, then apart. "I rammed my bicycle right into it and went flying. Cuts and bruises everywhere, and somehow managed to twist my ankle. And I bent the front wheel of the bike so badly that it couldn't be used. We weren't too far from Kampung Baru at the time. I was crying by then, so worried I wouldn't make it to safety, wouldn't make it back to my family." Her fingers never stop moving. "Your mother said we should walk. 'I'll help you,' she said. 'I won't leave you, Tipah. We'll make it in no time!'"

She pauses, and I feel as though my heart stops until she starts to speak again. "We weren't more than ten minutes away from Batu Road when we heard them." She swallows hard. "The Chinese mob, coming through Chow Kit to attack Kampung Baru. My heart stopped then. I knew that if they saw us, they'd kill us. And I couldn't run, not with my ankle. So I turned to your mother and I told her she had to run, to get away, as fast as she could. At least one of us would make it. But your mother refused." In the darkness within, the Djinn chuckles.

Auntie Tipah wipes away a tear from her cheek. "I could kill for a cigarette right now," she says, smiling shakily. Her hands tremble. In the time it takes for her to pick up her story again, Mama dies a million deaths in my head. "Anyway. We tried to hurry along, but the noises were getting closer and closer and she knew I couldn't go any faster. We were passing these abandoned houses, some all burned down, and she shoved me into this outhouse. Told me to keep the door shut and to be as still as I could. I told her,

'No, no, you have to hide too, where are you going?' But she just shushed me and told me to lock the door."

She takes a deep breath. "I thought then that she'd run far, far away, or at least go and hide. But no, not your mother. I peeked through the crack in the door and I saw her walk along for a little while, and then just stop. Like she was waiting for something. I thought to myself, *What in the world is Salmah doing?* And then I figured it out."

She looks at me then, finally, her smile achingly sad. "She wanted them to see her," she says quietly. "She wanted them to keep their eyes on her, to chase her if they wanted. She let herself be bait to lead them away so that they wouldn't find me."

She shuts her eyes then, and two more tears ooze out and trickle slowly down her cheeks; quickly, she fumbles about in the pocket of her wide skirt for a pale pink hand-kerchief to wipe them away. "I need a damn cigarette," she mumbles under her breath. I can feel my chest rising and falling convulsively; I'm having trouble sucking in air, and my pulse is starting to race in response. Somewhere within, the Djinn whistles a merry little tune.

"Did it work?" I manage to ask, at last.

She nods. "The mob ran past where I was, shivering with fear in the outhouse, trying my hardest not to scream. I heard them shouting, 'Who is that?' 'What is she up to?' I tried to see what was happening, but I couldn't. After a few minutes, everything was silent again." She half smiles. "That outhouse stank of piss and shit, but I stayed in there for what seemed like hours, even though I couldn't breathe without feeling like I was going to vomit. When I finally worked up the courage to open the door, I made my way to the main road and managed to hitch a ride here."

She falls silent then, her fingers spreading out and smoothing the little square of cotton over her lap, seemingly determined to rid it of every single blemish and wrinkle, and I stare down at my own feet and concentrate on tapping each of my big toes in counts of three, starting on the right, the better to swallow back my own tears.

"I'm sorry."

My head snaps up. "What?"

"I'm sorry," she says again, barely above a whisper; she's still looking down, and I see her hands tremble as they worry away at the little pink handkerchief. "She saved my life, and I have no idea where she is or what happened to her. I'm so sorry." A single tear falls onto the hankie, and as the Djinn screams obscene thoughts of my mother's death in my ears, I watch the moisture creep slowly across the fabric, rendering it sheer and fragile-looking—as thin as a spider's web.

CHAPTER TWELVE

IN THE CORRIDOR OUTSIDE THE hall, where brightly painted murals gambol across the walls in lurid technicolor, I sit with my back against a scene depicting a traditional Malay dance and try to capture the thoughts flying in all directions, like pieces of paper in a storm, and pin them down. Every once in a while, the Djinn waves his arms about, trying to distract me from the process. But I ignore him.

I think about how it felt to help Roslan back to his kampong, how it felt convincing those soldiers to help Jee. I try to remember what it felt like to be courageous. I beat the Djinn before. I can do it again.

I need to focus.

At this point, I decide, my options are:

A. Stay here, where it's safe and there's food and water readily available, or

B. Leave the guaranteed safety of this place to find Mama.

Any sane person would choose A. Any sane person

would reason that Mama, knowing those who are left without homes or places to turn to, would come here. Any sane person would opt to stay safe rather than take on gangs, soldiers, and who knows what else in the streets outside. *Choose A, Melati.*

Then again, any sane person doesn't spend sleepless nights counting in groups of three, go into conniptions at being unable to tap things, house djinns in their bodies, or imagine their own mother's death.

The only way I know I'll feel better is by being with Mama. And if out there is where Mama is, then I guess I'll just have to head out and find her.

B it is.

The decision made, I do my best to quash down the wave of panic and endless questions the Djinn starts firing into my head—*How? Where? What if you get hurt? Who will help you?* over and over again, like an increasingly screechy tune—and try to concentrate on formulating a plan.

I wish Vince were here.

So you can watch him get hurt again?

I tap quickly on the cold concrete floor to appease him. *Think, Melati, think.* The thoughts come sluggishly, as if they're swimming to the surface of a sea of sludge. I get up and start pacing, as though to help jog them along. How to get around the city? No buses. I can't drive. A bicycle, then. I'll commandeer a bicycle.

Good. Next step. Where to go? I frown, tapping my fingers incessantly against my left wrist, trying to concentrate, capture every thought. Mama was going from the hospital to Kampung Baru, from Kampung Baru to Petaling Street. Our home was burned down, and nobody saw her come back, so she must have headed to the cinema.

Okay. So that means that Mama is somewhere between home and Petaling Street.

Sure, the Djinn says agreeably. *Lying stiff and cold on the ground somewhere between home and Petaling Street.*

Shut up, I tell him fiercely. *Shut up.* And before he has the chance to say anything else, I head quickly for the door.

Time to steal a bicycle.

As it turns out, stealing a bicycle proves to be harder than I thought. Most people were shuttled over to the stadium in cars, ambulances, buses—safe, covered vehicles that made it harder to be pierced by blades or bullets.

Fair enough. But it does mean that I lack options.

I lean back against the wall, feeling defeated. *Thwarted before you even begin,* the Djinn says tauntingly. *Why not just head inside, curl up into a ball, and think about how you just let your mother die?*

I shake my head to shut him up, then grit my teeth. *Fine. I'll walk.*

The straightforward route along Davidson Road

won't do—the FRU soldiers are everywhere, patrolling along with their helmets and truncheons, and I can't take the risk of running into anyone. So I decide to cut through the smaller roads toward Chin Woo, then work my way around it and onto Petaling Street.

Okay. Deep breaths.

I wait until the guard patrolling the outside of the stadium turns the corner before dashing quickly across the parking lot, ducking behind trucks and cars as I go, my heart pounding in my ears, convinced I'm going to hear shots whizzing through the air at any minute. I have one big road to cross before I can get to Chin Woo; I can see the round building in the distance, the streetlights glinting on its many windows. *You'll never make it,* the Djinn whispers, but I quash him back down. I'm too busy for his nonsense right now. I need to focus.

Shooting looks left and right, I sprint across the road, keeping my body low, heading straight for the stadium. Then, wiping my damp hands on my skirt, I begin working my way slowly along the fence that hugs the back of the building, walking as quickly and quietly as I can, sticking close to the fence so I can take cover in its shadows. Behind the boards I hear the gentle slop and splash of water—*the pool,* I think to myself. I'm about to move on when I hear something else, something that makes me freeze.

A muffled scream from behind the fence.

Biting back a rising panic, I begin feeling along the fence wildly in the dim light, until my fingers hit on a gap between two boards big enough to peep through. I crouch down, getting up close, trying to make out what's happening.

A young girl—she looks to be about my age, in the white blouse and slightly-too-long green skirt that marks her as a student at the nearby Chinese school—is shrinking back against the opposite end of the fence, her eyes wide with fear, her arms outstretched as if to stop someone. I follow the direction of her gaze and see a man coming toward her, his back to me, dressed in full military gear. As I watch from my hiding place, he grabs her wrist roughly so that she yelps in pain, then covers her mouth with his other hand, forcing his body against hers. Her eyes close; even from where I am, I can see the tracks her tears have left on her cheeks.

I have to do something. I have to do something.

Barely even thinking, I grab a handful of rocks from the ground next to me, stand up, and in one smooth motion lob them with all my might over the fence. Then I crouch down again, the roaring in my ears so great at this point I can barely hear anything else at all. The Djinn screams a litany of death and doom in my ears, and I tap quietly against the fence. *One, two, three, one, two, three, one, two, three . . .*

The rocks land everywhere, some clattering on the

ground or on the wooden deck chairs surrounding the
pool, some with a splash in the water itself. The soldier
jumps back, his body tense and alert; the girl takes advan-
tage of the opportunity to wriggle out of his grasp and run
back into the safety of the hall. Swearing under his breath,
the soldier hoists his pack of gear back onto his shoulder
and makes his way after her.

I sag against the wooden boards, weak with relief, my
body drenched with sweat. It takes me a while to be able
to get up again, and when I do, my legs are so shaky that I
have to lean against the fence for support.

Keep going, I tell myself, *keep going. You need to get
to Mama. Keep going.*

A few minutes later, I'm back on Petaling Street. Bathed in
moonlight, the streets are eerily silent and empty, the bodies that littered the roads and sidewalks just days before
having been, I assume, carted off to the morgue by now.
Okay, Melati. You made it. Where do we go from here?

I keep my eyes open, darting glances up and down the
street as I think. *If Mama came here looking for me, she'd
head straight for the Rex*, I tell myself. *So that's where I
have to go.*

Immediately, the Djinn shrieks in protest. *The Rex?
Don't you remember what happened at the Rex, Melati?*
He conjures up images of Saf's pale, tearstained face, that

emerges with a dark blue blanket. "Here, take this." The blanket is soft and worn with multiple washings, and I wrap it around myself gratefully, luxuriating in the warmth. "Now," he says, leaning back in his seat and smoothing his mustache, "what was that about your mother?"

"I'm trying to find her," I say. "She left work when all the . . . troubles . . . started, and she came to Petaling Street to look for me and bring me home. But we never found each other, and now I don't know where she is. . . ." My voice trails off, and I suddenly feel very, very tired.

The officer is silent, contemplating my words. Then he nods. "Right. Well, she might certainly be here," he says, gesturing to the hallway. "Lots of people taking shelter here for a bit until everything dies down. It's the safest place to be around here. Why don't we go take a look? Hakim!" he barks to a younger officer in the back room, who comes running. "Yes, sir?"

"Keep an eye on things here while I try to help this young lady."

"Yes, sir." Hakim takes his place at the desk, and the officer comes around to where I stand. "Thank you, Officer . . ." "You can call me Pakcik Hassan," he says, smiling at me paternally. "Now come, let's see if we can find your mother."

He leads me down a hallway with doors on either side that open to reveal rooms filled with more people. I go

last imploring look before the doors closed. *You stood back and did nothing. You didn't protect your friend. You saved your own skin and you let her die. It was your fault. Your fault. All your fault.*

His accusations come thick and fast; the guilt floods through me, knocking me to my knees and leaving me gasping for breath. At that moment, I spot two bright lights in the distance; headlights. I need to run, I need to hide. But my limbs are heavy and I can't move.

The headlights are coming steadily closer, and I can just make it out: an FRU truck. *Move, Melati. Move. You need to move.* There is no way I can get back on my feet, so I crawl as quickly as I can from the pavement into the burned-out shophouse closest to me, wedging myself between a blackened wall and a pile of rubble. I try to stay my loud, rasping breath, but I can't seem to stop panting. I focus on the rubble beside me and try to count the number of bricks I can see, squinting to make them out in the dim line. Three, six, nine, twelve, fifteen, eighteen, twenty-one . . . I stay here counting long after the rumble of the FRU truck has faded into the night, until my breathing is even again. I know I should leave, start making my way to the Rex, find my mother, but the Djinn has me in his bony, unyielding grasp, and I can't make myself move, can't do anything but count and count and count and count and count.

I'm at 1,425 when I fall asleep, curled up on the cold concrete floor.

I awaken as the pale, gray light of early dawn steals into my hiding place. I unfold myself and do my best to rub some feeling back into my cold, stiff limbs. My stomach rumbles, and I try to remember when I had my last meal. Yesterday? Was it breakfast? Lunch? And I have nothing with me to eat or drink now. I lick my dry lips and sigh. *You really didn't think this through, Melati.*

Mercifully, the Djinn is silent this morning, and I work up the courage to peek outside, where a steady, light drizzle seems to strip the city of color, turning everything lifeless and gray. I feel goose bumps rising on my arms and quickly wrap them around myself to ward off the sudden chill in my bones. *What do I do now?*

The quiet of the early morning is shattered. A siren blares in the distance, and in the next moment a police car comes barreling down the road, its tires screeching as it turns the corner and roars off.

Of course! The police station! It's a big one, just a few minutes away. I breathe a sigh of relief; I know people have been taking shelter in police stations, so my mother might be there. And if she isn't, well, they're policemen— they can tell me what to do.

Feeling better than I have in a long time, I run quickly

out of the shophouse and down the lanes and alleyway toward the police station. The rain trickles down my hai and pools in the hollows of my collarbones and in the bot toms of my shoes so that I make squelching sounds wit each step, but I don't care. Finally, finally, I feel like I ca see an end to this whole ordeal. I'll find my mother, ar everything will be right again.

The station looms high over the rest of Petaling Stre painted in the signature blue and white colors of the pol force. I make my way inside, pushing open the heavy do and leaving a trail of water on the tiled floor as I l around for someone to speak to. Inside, the station is of people, but relatively calm; men, women, and chil sit on benches or on the floor, talking quietly or not a One little girl cuddling close to her dozing mother l up at me with frank curiosity in her eyes, her hands cl ing an old rag doll with one missing eye and a frayed

I head straight for the front desk, where an o barely looks up as I approach, busily writing in som before him. "Yes?" he says brusquely.

"Hello, sir," I say politely. "I'm looking for my m

He looks up properly then, taking me in, in shivering, drenched, bedraggled glory, my soaked ur clinging to me like a second skin. His expression s "Child, you must be freezing!" he says, turning and rummaging in some cupboards behind him u

through each one, combing through the faces hungrily for my mother's familiar smile. But the more rooms we go through without finding her, the more my heart drops, and by the time we finish it's all the way in the depths of my shoes, soaking in the dirty rainwater at my feet.

"Well," Pakcik Hassan says, then stops, unsure how to continue. I can't speak; I just stare morosely at the ground and listlessly count the scuffed tiles on the floor around us.

He clears his throat and tries again. "Well. You must be hungry. Everything always looks better with some food in your stomach. You sit here and I'll get you something." He points me in the direction of an empty chair, and I drag my feet over to it and sit. I'm still counting, for lack of anything better to do, but mostly I just feel numb.

Pakcik Hassan returns bearing a bun and a cup filled with steaming black coffee. I nibble at the bun, which is soft and tasteless. I don't normally drink coffee—I can't stand the bitter aftertaste—but gulp it down anyway. The hot liquid burns my tongue and throat, but wakes me up, for which I'm grateful. "I'm sorry she isn't here, child," Pakcik Hassan says gently, watching me. "I'm sure she's safe somewhere. We know there are people taking shelter in the temples, the churches, the mosques, in schools. She could be with a friend in someone's house. Plenty of places. Why don't you stay here, wait it out? Once it's safer and we get the all clear, we can take you home."

I nod, and eventually he walks away, back to his post at the front desk. I sit there for what seems like an age, not thinking of anything in particular, just taking in my surroundings. On the wall across from where I sit, a little brown lizard makes its way determinedly from one side to the other, darting across in fits and starts, pausing anytime it spots some perceived, unknown danger to wait and watch before proceeding. A journey that could have taken a minute or two stretches on and on—five minutes, ten minutes, fifteen . . .

Okay, universe. I get it.

I wrap the half-eaten bun up carefully in my handkerchief and stuff it into my backpack, fold the blanket as best I can, and leave it on my seat, balancing the coffee cup on top of it. Then I straighten myself up, take a deep breath, and stride toward the door. I'm going to find my mother if it kills me.

Or her, the djinn whispers.

I'm ignoring you.

But as soon as he sees me head for the door, Pakcik Hassan is up from his position behind the desk. "Where are you going?" he asks me pleasantly.

"I'm going to find my mother," I say, a little taken aback. He was watching me the whole time?

"Can't let you do that, child," he says, stroking his mustache. "Too dangerous. You stay put here and we'll take care of you."

"But, Pakcik—"

He shakes his head firmly. "No, no. I have a daughter about your age and I'll be damned if I'd ever let her be out and about at a time like this. No, you stay here, and we'll sort everything out later, when it's safe."

By later, it'll be too late! The Djinn hisses the words, pacing restlessly in the pit of my stomach; I tap my right pointer finger against the palm of my left hand and itch to push open the doors and run out. But I know it's no use; Pakcik Hassan will just haul me back inside. Instead, I walk away, keeping the exit within sight. The minute I spot my chance, I decide, I'm making a break for it.

It doesn't take long. The doors burst open, slamming hard against the walls. It's a young Chinese man, his eyes wild with rage. "You killed my mother! You killed my mother, you useless dogs!" His hair is disheveled, his cheeks are grubby with dirt and tears, and his hands grip a short, sharp knife, which swings and stabs wildly through the air with every gesture.

Pakcik Hassan and the young Hakim leap to their feet immediately. "Calm down, sir, please calm down."

"I will not calm down! All she was doing was standing in our garden! She didn't even know there was a curfew on and you bloody fools shot her in cold blood! You and your stupid shoot-to-kill order."

His knees buckle and he sinks to the floor, as if bowing

to the weight of his own grief. "She never even killed spiders or cockroaches," he says quietly. "She fed every stray cat or dog or human she ever met. How could you do that to her? How could you?" He throws the knife across the room, where it lands with a clang and skids across the floor, stopping right by my feet. I stare at it; it's a pearl-handled pocket knife, the kind with a blade that slips in, out of sight. Before I can figure out what I'm doing it, I bend over, scoop it up, flip it shut, and slip it smoothly into the pocket of my skirt in one swift movement, my heart jangling urgently inside my chest. I look around to see if anyone has noticed, but all eyes are firmly on the weeping man.

The officers standing over him exchange glances. As they whisper urgently with each other, trying to figure out what to do next, I slip quietly out the doors and sprint down the road, the knife weighing down my skirt and bumping against my thigh. As I run, the Djinn pipes up over the pounding of my feet on the pavement. *That could be you, you know.*

Shut up, I tell him, silently counting the beat of my footsteps in comforting, solid threes. I don't want to admit that I was just thinking the exact same thing.

The temple is just minutes from the police station; I've often stopped as I passed to drink in the intricate carvings and statues that adorn its towering façade. Everywhere you look, gods and deities dance and gambol and grin and leer, all rendered in brilliant, vivid hues and studded with gems. As I step through the arch, I feel a strange sense of passing from one realm into another. It's quiet on the streets outside, but that's a quiet charged with a hostile undercurrent, an uneasy tension that calls for constant vigilance. In here the floor is cool, the scent of incense floats delicately in the air, and the quiet is calm and serene. Under the staring eyes of a thousand idols, even the Djinn is silent.

Mama often tells me to seek God, to invoke His name, ask for His help. I bow my head and obey, the familiar words for Dzikr rolling off my tongue, the motions for prayer smooth and ready. God is good, they teach us. God is great. God can heal the sick and soothe the tormented. But nobody seems to be able to tell me why God gave me this torment in the first place.

I'm sure God exists, I'm just not sure He likes me very much.

"Can I help you?"

The voice, deep and even, catches me off guard and I whirl around in surprise. The man has smiling eyes and a face half-hidden behind a well-tended forest of facial hair; dressed in a loose cotton shirt and pants, he looks cool, calm, and completely untouched by the chaos of the past week. I am suddenly painfully aware of how grubby I must look in my rumpled and damp clothes.

"I'm sorry for intruding," I say. "I've been trying to find my mother. We lost each other on the day . . . the day the . . . you know." I can't bring myself to speak of such things in this peaceful place; it almost seems sacrilegious.

The man nods. "Yes, many people came for shelter here when it was happening," he says. "I'm not sure why! We don't even have any doors to shut people out. But even without doors, there are not many who would attempt to desecrate this place with violence or angry words."

"Was my mother here?" I ask him eagerly. "She's a nurse. Her name is Salmah. She came to Petaling Street looking for me, but we missed each other. . . . Have you seen her?"

He frowns, trying to remember. Then his brow clears, and he smiles. "Salmah! Yes, I do remember Nurse Salmah."

"You do?" I hardly dare to hope at this point—my heart has been let down far too many times by far too many people.

"Yes, yes, Nurse Salmah in her white uniform. She was taking the time to check everyone who walked in, to make sure they were not badly hurt, or to treat them if they were. A wonderful woman."

I smile. "That sounds like my mother, all right. Is she . . . is she here?"

His smile fades, and he shakes his head. "No, she did not stay. She was intent on finding her daughter, you see. You."

Another wall to slam into, just when I thought there was hope. I want to cry. *Shake it off, Melati, shake it off.* "As long as we're both working hard to find each other, I'm sure we will. Thank you, sir, for your time." As I walk back through the doorway, I can feel the man's eyes on me, and an overwhelming urge to stay awhile and let my soul, so used to noise and chaos, feed on the peace of the temple.

No, I tell myself sternly. *Mama needs you.*

And so I force myself to keep striding on down the road, never turning back to see the gods smiling down on me.

I concentrate, putting one foot in front of the other, determined to continue my search. *The church next,* I think to myself, *then that mosque a little farther down the road. That's where I should go next.* But my feet seem to have minds of their own, and each step I take that propels me farther from the temple seems to take me closer to the Rex instead. *This doesn't make sense, Melati. Mama wouldn't be waiting for you in a cinema when there are so many safer options out here.* But I can't shake the feeling that the Rex is calling to me, shining a beacon to pull me in its direction.

The closer I get, the louder and more hectoring the Djinn's voice becomes. *Ready to see what happens when you're a selfish coward?* He sends image after image shooting into my mind: Saf slumped low in a theater seat, her arms splayed awkwardly; Saf with blood trickling from the gaping stab wound in her chest; Saf, staring at my retreating back, her eyes wide with fear and betrayal. *Your mother's next. She came looking for you and she'll pay the price for it. Everybody pays a price for loving you.*

I duck and weave and dart through empty shophouses, behind and between the charred carcasses of buses and cars, trying to avoid the keen glances of patrolling soldiers, counting in threes and tapping my tongue against my teeth as I go to silence that wicked voice.

And then, finally, I'm here.

The Rex.

Some of the brightly colored posters have been ripped off the walls, and the pavement before it is littered with both kuaci shells and dark stains that look suspiciously like blood. But otherwise, the bright red block letters stand as tall as ever, and Paul Newman's piercing blue eyes gaze soulfully from the one poster that remains intact by the main entrance. "It was a hell of a story, Paul," I whisper to him before I push against the heavy double doors.

Inside, the only relief from darkness comes from the sunlight that filters weakly in through the dusty windows. Beneath my feet, the floor is littered with debris; I can't see exactly what I'm stepping on, but I feel the crunch. As I walk toward the doors leading to the movie hall, my foot lands on something that rolls beneath its weight, sending me toppling to the floor with a shriek. I feel around with my hands (it's the usher's flashlight), evaluate my injuries (a bruised tailbone and a heart pitter-pattering erratically from the shock), then get up, dusting myself off.

"Let's try this," I murmur, pushing the button on the flashlight. It's a small one, nestling in my palm just so, but its beam is bright and true, and I feel myself daring to breathe again. It's amazing how reassured you can feel just by the presence of light.

Armed with my flashlight, I turn to face the movie hall. *Here's where the magic happens!* The Djinn resurfaces, and I can see his lazy grin as we contemplate the closed doors. *What if they're all still in there?* He uses my heart to bang out a fast and furious drum sequence; the pounding is almost more than I can bear. *What if they didn't collect these bodies?*

I can feel my body tighten, my hands clenching themselves into fists. I can't walk through this door. I can't.

Maybe I should check the rest of the theater first. That's reasonable, right? That makes sense. If Mama came here, she could be anywhere. She doesn't necessarily have to be behind those doors, in that hall.

So I turn away from the doors, barely containing the sigh of relief that escapes me, and start combing through the rest of the building. I shine my light into the box office, where bits of paper are scattered all over the countertops;

I search the snack bar, where someone has spilled an entire vat of the sickly sweet orange cordial they sell to quench moviegoers' thirst; I even sidle into a door clearly marked EMPLOYEES ONLY, feeling a spark of rebellion as I peer inside. There are stacks of papers and files, but no Mama.

Every place I search that comes up empty takes me one step closer to the inevitable: the movie hall. Even thinking about it makes the Djinn stir restlessly and my pulse quicken.

And then he begins throwing questions at me, relentless, like bullets. *What if Saf was just wounded, but you were too much of a coward to come back for her and so she died, in pain and alone? What if Mama came to look for you here and ended up coming face-to-face with the gangsters who murdered Saf? What if they murdered her, too?*

Quickly, I begin to pace: three steps at a time, first to one side, then to the other. Then I tap each corner of the door frame three times, then each handle. I can't seem to get it right, so I set the flashlight aside, making sure to keep the beam pointing toward the door. Then I begin again, over and over and over again. Step, tap, step, tap, counting every time. I'm sweaty and shaky, and I feel like I may throw up, but I can't get around it—I can't step through these doors until it feels right. Until it feels safe.

Somewhere inside me, the Djinn reclines luxuriously and chuckles to himself.

I hate him.

I hate me.

It must be more than twenty minutes before I can finally, finally push the doors open.

It's all there, just as it's always been: the wooden seats; the big screen at the very front of the room, now blank and gray; and in the middle of the hall, the one lone seat covered in bright red cloth. The spirit of the Rex. Whoever he is, he certainly isn't alone now.

I stand there at the threshold, taking it all in. How many movies have I watched here, giggling with Saf as we sipped on sweet sugarcane juice and crunched through handfuls of nuts? I close my eyes, the image of Saf's dimpled smile playing in my mind. The air here has the stale quality you only get from a room that's been sealed off from the rest of the world for a while, and I'm suddenly finding it hard to breathe. I sink into the closest chair, and the creak as my weight rests on it echoes deafeningly in the silent hall.

Deep breaths, Melati.

Out of habit, I find myself counting them off—*breathe in, one, two, three, breathe out, one, two, three, breathe in, one, two, three*—and then I hear it.

The soft but unmistakable sound of an answering creak.

I freeze, straining my ears to hear it again. There—

another little creak. I reach into my pocket, my fingers stroking the smooth handle of the little knife.

"Who's there?" I call out, and immediately regret it. *How stupid can you be, Melati? A city full of hostile riot-ers, and you call attention to yourself like this?* But even though I wait and wait, there's no response. For one wild moment, I wonder if the spirit is real, and after my journey through the city I'm about to be murdered by a vengeful ghost.

Then I hear it again—and something else. Light, quick footsteps, so light you would barely notice them, if you weren't really listening.

Immediately, I spring up out of my seat, as light as a cat, and sprint out of the door and up the stairs to the first-class section, two by two, knife in one hand, torch in the other. I know I may be putting myself in danger, I know there's no real way of knowing what I'll find up there, but for some reason I'm driven by a powerful urge to see it for myself. *For some reason?* The Djinn scoffs. *Please. You think it might be Saf. You think she's somehow alive and waiting for you.*

Shut up.

The upper tier is closed off to the rest of the world by a heavy wooden door, and as I hesitate before it, I think of all the times Saf and I schemed and hatched elaborate plots to make our way through it and take our seats high above the rest of the commoners. Slowly, I push the door open.

Rows of seats stretch out before me, just the same as the ones downstairs. I play my torch along their wooden spines and feel a little pang of disappointment. We'd always imagined something grander: velvet seats, plush carpets underfoot, intricate murals painted along the walls. It turns out that all "first-class" means is a different point of view and marginally cleaner floors.

Slowly, I scan my torch across the space. I'm not sure what I expect to see, but since nobody's come out and attacked me yet, I figure I'm pretty safe. Maybe it was just a rat.

And then the beam of light lands on something unexpected, and I pause.

Rats don't wear shoes.

These are small and pale pink, though caked in parts with grime and flecked with stains. Little pink-and-white polka dot bows adorn the tops. And the feet encased in them belong to a little girl, no older than seven or eight, I'm guessing, crouched low at the very end of the third row, her eyes squinting in the bright light of the torch, every muscle poised to flee.

I soften immediately—I know what that feels like. "Hello," I say, turning the beam away so that it doesn't blind her, flicking the knife shut and putting it away. I make my voice as soft and gentle as I can. "Hello there. Are you all right? Are you hurt?"

The little girl shrinks back even farther, so that her back touches the wall. "Don't be afraid. I won't hurt you." I inch my way closer to her, trying to make my movements as slow and deliberate as I can, as if I'm approaching some kind of wild animal. "What's your name? My name is Melati. You can call me kakak. Do you know what that means? It means 'big sister.'"

"I'm . . . I'm May," she says, her voice barely above a whisper and cracking from disuse.

"Well, hi, May, it's nice to meet you. Can I come and sit by you?"

She hesitates, then nods, and I quickly make my way over and sit cross-legged beside her, my back against the wall.

"Are you alone here, May?"

She nods, her big eyes never leaving my face.

"Okay. How long have you been here?" I have a million questions, but I know I can't rush her, and I force myself to ask one at a time.

She shrugs. I take in her crusty face, the discarded food wrappers and beverage containers piled neatly in the nearby corner. She's been scavenging from the snack bar, I realize, hiding in here while the chaos raged outside.

"Was there anybody else here when you came in?" I ask softly. She shakes her head. "I was with my mummy," she volunteers timidly. "We were buying tea at the tea uncle's shop. She said she needed a special kind of tea because my daddy wasn't feeling well."

I nod encouragingly. "That's right; there are teas that can help people feel better. Then what happened?"

"There was a lot of banging and shouting suddenly. I don't know what happened. The tea shop uncle said he had to close the shop. He told Mummy to stay in the back room with me and keep quiet until he said we could come out. Mummy said it was like a game. So I stayed really super quiet because I like to win."

I swallow a sudden lump in my throat. "I'm sure you're very good at games," I say, and she nods vigorously. "I am," she tells me solemnly. "I always beat my mummy at checkers and snakes and ladders." She pauses, then adds reluctantly, "I think she lets me win at checkers, though. But only sometimes."

"I'm sure there are lots of times when you beat her fair and square." I smile at her. "What happened after that?"

She frowns. "Mummy kept peeking through the door to see what was happening. There was a lot more noise outside, more crashing and banging, so I thought we'd win for sure because the uncle was being so loud. Then Mummy grabbed me and told me we had to leave. The back room had a door that could let you out, so she used that, and then we ran away. I was mad because Mummy carried me just like a baby, and I am NOT a baby anymore. Mummy said I wasn't fast enough. But I am! I can run really, really fast." She scowls deeply at the indignity of it all.

"I bet you can," I say, and she relaxes a little. "Is that how you ended up here?"

She nods firmly. "When we came in, there were lots of people sleeping in the chairs downstairs. Mummy said they were so tired from watching the movie. We stayed in a room downstairs and Mummy would lock the door and put a chair in front of it. The floor was soo hard, I couldn't sleep properly and I really wanted to go home. But I did get to eat all kinds of yummy snacks Mummy doesn't usually let me buy. . . ." She trails off, contemplating the pros and cons of cinema life.

"Where'd your mummy go?" I ask her gently. Her face falls. "There was a lot of loud noises outside, so she went to go see. She said I had to stay quiet and hide in our room and not let anyone inside at all. She said it was like another game. And if she didn't come back, if I won, then someone would come find me and bring me home." She looks down then. "I cheated, though. I got hungry, so I had to come out." Her lips tremble slightly as she looks up at me. "Can I still win? Are you going to take me home?" she asks.

My heart wrenches. I can't leave her here to fend for herself.

Everybody who's around you gets hurt, the Djinn says warningly. *You're toxic, Melati. You're capable of protect-*

ing nothing and no one. You'll get this girl killed, just like you got Saf killed. The mention of Saf's name sends a stabbing pain shooting through my chest, and I waver for an instant.

Then I feel a little hand work its way into mine. May looks up at me trustingly, and I know right then that there is no way I'm leaving without her. "That's right," I tell her. "I'm going to get you out of here, and we'll find a way to get you home."

And I squeeze her hand and smile reassuringly at her as the Djinn screams and scenes of death swirl around my head.

So I haven't found Mama, and I've managed to saddle myself with a child that I'm somehow supposed to cart around the city while I look for her.

You, Melati, are a fine, fine fool.

I sigh and look down at May, who is sitting on a bench in the lobby munching contentedly on the bun I'd managed to fish out of my bag.

The bun. The bun that I'd gotten from the police station. That's it! The police station isn't too far away; I'll take May there. She'll be safe, they'll be able to get her back home, and I'll slip away again when they aren't looking and go find Mama on my own.

Satisfied with my plan, I kneel down so I'm eye level

with the girl. "May, we're going to get you to the police station, okay? The uncles there will know how to get you home." She looks at me with those big brown eyes and nods. Her hand hasn't left mine.

When she's done eating, I take her to the bathroom to wash up. "Do you need to go?" I ask her, hearing echoes of my own mother. She nods and slips into one of the stalls. While waiting, I stare blankly at my own reflection. This entire situation feels unreal.

The sound of the flushing toilet echoes through the tiny bathroom, and she opens the door and steps out. The yellow dress she wears is a touch too long for her, and I imagine I can hear her mother's voice parroting what all mothers say: *Better to make it big, so she can wear it for a long time more.* All it does is make her look even smaller, more vulnerable than she already is. I suddenly want to hug her.

Instead, I lead her to the sink and help her wash the worst of the smudges and smears off her face. Then we head back out to the lobby.

"Okay," I say, looking down to make sure she's listening. "We don't really know what it's like out there, so you need to listen to me and do what I tell you, okay?" She nods, her little face serious. "If I tell you to run, you run. If I tell you to stay still, you be as quiet as you can be. Okay?" Another nod, and she slips her hand firmly back into mine and clutches it as though she's never letting go.

"Okay. Stay close to me." I take a deep breath. "Here we go."

Slowly, carefully, I push open the heavy theater doors and glance up and down the street. All is quiet. "Come on," I say, tugging at May's hand, and we run quickly up the street, staying close to the wall. At the intersection of Cecil and Petaling Street I turn right—and then abruptly shove the little girl behind a blue Ford Anglia abandoned by the side of the street, the door on the driver's side hanging wide open, its windshield an intricate mass of cracks spawning from a hole almost right in the center of the glass, where a rock has smashed through. "Get in, get in," I hiss at her, and crawl in behind her, swinging the door shut behind me as quietly as I can. Then we both peek over the Ford's pale leather seats at the scene behind us.

Just ahead, men are busy smashing the windows and doors of the shops that line Petaling Street with large rocks and rods of iron and wood. They force their way in, pushing back metal shutters and wooden gates, and exit bearing armfuls of loot: food and provisions, transistor radios and television sets, fistfuls of money that they stuff into pockets and bags. As we watch, one man lights a cigarette, then tosses his still-lit match casually in through a broken window; minutes later, fire crackles merrily in the empty building, sending cascades of smoke billowing into the sky. The others pause to roar their approval.

Beside me, I can feel May's whole body trembling, and I hug her close. "Don't worry," I whisper in her ear. "They won't find us. I'll keep us safe."

She curls into me and stays there quietly while I frantically try and figure out what to do next. There are only two roads we can take to the police station; Petaling Street is out, and if we cross over and try to head up Jalan Bandar, we run the risk of them seeing us, especially with May, who can't run as fast or as far as I can. I sigh in frustration; I can't see any way around them, and time is running out. We can't stay here forever.

Think, Melati, think. This kid is depending on you.

For all the good that will do her. The Djinn decides that this would be a good time to pipe up. In my head, the movie reel clicks into place: Mama and Saf and May and Vince atop a pile of bodies in the lobby of the Rex, bloodied and bloated from all the days they've been left to rot, waiting for me to find them, protect them, save them.

I tap my fingers rapidly against my palm, shaking my head as if I can somehow put my thoughts back in place. May's watchful eyes peer up at me questioningly, but she stays quiet.

If she stays with you, she'll just end up getting hurt. They all do.

"Kakak?"

I open my eyes to see May staring at me, confused and

frightened. And well she should be—there's a riot going on behind us and all her supposed protector can do is sit in a car with her eyes shut.

She needs you, Melati. Get a grip.

"It's okay, May," I say, trying to smile at her as reassuringly as I can. "We're going to slip out and run as fast as we can down that road over there, okay? You see that big white van over there?" I point to where the abandoned van sits, a few yards down the road from us. "When I say go, you run to that van and hide behind it, okay? I'll hold your hand the whole time, but you have to run as hard as you can. Can you do that for me?" She nods, biting her bottom lip so hard I can see a drop of blood.

"Good girl. Are you ready?"

She hesitates, and my heart constricts. "You can do it. I'll be with you the whole time, okay? I won't leave you."

"Okay, kakak," she whispers.

"Okay, let's go."

I grip the little hand tightly in mine and slowly open the door, inch by inch, shooting glances behind me as I go. *Please don't see us, please don't see us, please don't see us.*

One deep breath. Then I tug at May's hand, hiss "Go!", and run, trying to keep my body low, my hair streaming behind me. I swear I hear footsteps pounding behind us, but I don't dare look back. The van. The van. Just make it to the van. Beside me, May struggles valiantly to keep up, her hand clutching mine so tightly it's almost numb.

It seems like it takes us forever to cover the distance from one hiding spot to another, but finally we sink to the ground behind the white van, panting hard. I crouch to peek out from beneath the van and see if anyone has noticed us, but other than the commotion from Petaling Street, we seem to be alone.

"And where do you think you're going, girlie?"

I swing around, shoving May behind me, my heart in my throat.

We aren't alone.

The man's voice is low and harsh, his English tinged with the lilt of a Chinese accent. His dark hair is cropped close to his head; his face bears a thin scar from chin to cheek; his dark blue shirt reeks of sweat and smoke. In one hand, he swings an iron pipe; in the other, a cigarette. *Dangerous*, the Djinn whispers, *he's dangerous.*

"Nowhere," I say. "We're just trying to get to our family."

The man takes one last drag, then flicks his cigarette to the ground. "Little girls playing in the streets at a time like this. Not very proper, is it? You ought to be punished." He grins at me, and I reach into my pocket, tapping the smooth handle of the little knife. One, two, three, one, two, three, one, two, three.

He'll hurt you. He'll hurt both of you.

"Just kidding. Can't take a joke, eh?"

Still, I don't speak. May buries her head into my back, and I do my best to block her little body with mine as much as I can. Hidden in my pocket, my fingers don't stop moving.

She's going to die because you did this, Melati. You led her into this situation, and now she's going to die.

"Cat got your tongue, little girl?"

He looms closer and closer and the Djinn's voice is echoing in my head and suddenly the knife is out and I'm slashing wildly, blindly. I don't even know what I'm doing; my vision is blurred and my breathing is labored and my ears are ringing, but the moment blade makes contact, I feel it: a sudden, visceral thrill. In my head, I hear Abah's voice: "That's right, Melati, that's how you hold it, wrap your fingers around the handle like this, your thumb like this. Good."

I was always handy with a knife.

The man reels back, his face a mask of shock, blood trickling from the shallow wound on his left arm. "You're crazy, you stupid girl!" he shouts, then turns and walks away, shaking his head.

The Djinn smiles a slow, delighted smile.

The knife falls to the ground, and I realize it's because my fingers are trembling so hard that it's slipped right out of my hand. I kick it away, as hard as I can, and it goes flying off into the streets.

May sidles over to me, and I hug her close. The heat is oppressive, yet somehow I can't stop shivering. "We have to get to a safe place," I tell her. I look up and down the streets, mentally trying to clear the chaos in my head, map our location, figure out where to go. Then I spot it. The school.

School, I think. *We could head for the school. There might be teachers there, adults who can protect us. There's nothing to steal at a school. Nobody has any reason to attack a school.*

I nudge May. "See that building over there?" She looks in the direction I'm pointing and nods. "That's a school. We're going to go there, okay?" She nods again. "Come on," I tell her. "Let's go."

We walk briskly, keeping close to walls and ducking low behind cars or trucks when we can. I hold May's hand and focus on putting one foot in front of the other, counting off in threes, and not on the look on the man's face, or the blood dripping down his arm, or the way it felt when the knife sliced into his flesh.

The school sprawls before us, seemingly untouched by the chaos that's raged around it for the past few days. This is an independent high school, reserved for the wealthy Chinese who want only the best for their children. Unlike most regular schools, including mine, this school is all solid brick and concrete and has the shiny, brand-new look of a building whose administrators can afford its upkeep.

The heavy iron gate is chained and padlocked, but the fence isn't too high, and I manage to hoist May up and over it, then clamber over myself, landing on the ground feetfirst. "Let's go inside," I say, dusting myself off and reaching for her hand. "Maybe there's someone here who can help us."

Cautiously, we step into the wide, paved corridors, relishing the cool relief that seems to emanate from the concrete walls. I pull May toward what seems to be the school hall. "Come on over here," I say. "If there's anyone here, that's where they're bound to . . ." The words die on my lips.

Down the corridor, a woman is approaching us. The lines of her dark dress are severe, her hair is scraped back into a bun, her lips are set in a thin, hard line, and her hands grip a heavy wooden bat.

The Djinn stirs immediately, wrapping his cold fingers around the base of my spine.

May gasps and instinctively, I push her behind me, shielding her body with mine, quickly tapping a protective tattoo along her little back as the Djinn whips my insides into a frenzied panic.

"Who are you?" the woman asks loudly, her voice echoing in the corridor. "What are you doing here?"

"Please, ma'am," I say, my arms outstretched, palms

up, trying to show her I have no weapons, I mean no harm. Beads of sweat are forming on my forehead and dripping slowly down my face, but I make no move to wipe them away. "Please, we're only looking for help. I have this little girl with me; we don't mean any harm. We're just looking for a safe place to hide."

There's nowhere to hide, the Djinn sneers. *There's no way for you to protect her. There's no way you can pull this off.* It takes effort, and I can feel my fingers spasm, longing to tap, to count, to do something, but I ignore him.

"How do I know you're not a trap?" the woman says harshly. "How do I know you haven't lead the looters and the thugs in to murder us all?"

"Please, ma'am," I say again. I can hear the note of desperation in my voice. "Please, this isn't any kind of trap. I just wanted to bring her somewhere safe." A sob escapes me before I can stop it. Behind me, May begins to cry, her little face buried in my back.

The woman relaxes her stance then, dropping her arms to her sides, a look of relief on her face.

"Sorry, girl," she says, her voice softening as she looks at May. "Sorry, sorry. It's been a difficult few days and we have people to protect. Cannot be too careful."

She beckons to us. "Come, come. I take you inside, we have food and water. You can rest."

My knees almost buckle with relief. May still clutches

my waist tightly and won't let me go, so I scoop her up in my arms and carry her like a baby. She flings her arms around my neck and hides her face in my shoulder, and I give her gentle pats on the back as I walk—one, two, three, one, two, three. I hum as I go, softly in her ear for only the two of us to hear. The girl with kaleidoscope eyes. She isn't the lightest, but unless my arms give out, I know there is no way I'm putting her down.

The woman—"Call me Miss Low," she barks over her shoulder as she walks briskly ahead of us—leads us through a maze of corridors and up flights of stairs until she finally stops short in front of a wooden door on the top floor. She pauses to tap lightly on it—three times, and I'm both pleased by this and ashamed at how pleased I am—before flinging it open.

We step into what seems to be a small library. Shoes are lined neatly along the wall next to the doorway, so as not to scuff the wooden floor. The walls are lined with worn, beat-up shelves filled with worn, beat-up old books. Light streams in from the windows that line the right-hand wall.

In the center of the room sits a small group of six or seven children. I can tell from the way they're seated around the teacher, who has a book in her hand, that she's been reading them a story; the sound of the door has put them all on alert, however, and all of their eyes are trained unblinkingly on us, their bodies tense and poised to flee.

May peeks out from behind me, and I give her hand a reassuring squeeze.

"Students," Miss Low says, her voice like a gunshot in the quiet room. "Students, we have some guests. These are . . ." She looks at me and quirks an eyebrow questioningly. "Melati," I supply. "And this is May," I add quickly.

"Very good. And what do we say, students?"

"Good afternoon, Melati and May," the children sing-song to us in unison, and I almost want to laugh.

Then I notice them. In the far corner of the room, a cot has been set up, and a child lies upon it, eyes shut and pale. A woman has been busily tending to him as we've been speaking, her back to us, but now she stands very erect and absolutely still.

"Puan?" I'm not the only one who's noticed; Miss Low is staring at the other woman, her brow furrowed. "Puan? Everything all right over there?"

Slowly, the woman turns, and suddenly the room seems to spin and whirl around me, as if I were the eye of some kind of surreal tornado.

"Melati?"

I blink rapidly, trying to clear the tears from my eyes.

"Hi, Mama."

CHAPTER THIRTEEN

I CAN'T BELIEVE THIS IS real.

I can't believe this is real.

Is this real? For a minute I waver. There have been long stretches in the past few days where I've been sure that I'm just in some bizarre, unending nightmare, that I'll wake up and Mama will be scolding me for blasting my records so loudly that Makcik Siti stopped by to complain about my "heathen music."

But no, I can feel Mama's arms around me, the soft fabric of her nurse's uniform against my cheek, the salty wetness of her tears on my neck. She's here. I did it; I found her. This is real.

I sink into her arms like I'm five years old again. "Where have you been?" she murmurs into my hair over and over again, clutching me tightly. "Where have you been? I've been out of my mind with worry." But I can't reply. I just want to stay here for as long as I can.

"Hurm." A dry, inquiring little half cough breaks the

spell, and we both turn our tear-streaked faces to see Miss Low looking at us, half-disapproving at this wanton display of emotion. Mama reluctantly lets me go, and I straighten my clothes, feeling as chastened as if I've just been caught cheating.

"I take it this is your daughter?" she says, and Mama nods. "Yes, and I'm just so relieved. I was looking for her, as you know, when I ended up here."

"How did you end up here?" I ask her.

"I was walking toward Petaling Street to look for you," Mama says, taking my hand and squeezing it tightly. "But as I was passing the school, I saw someone shouting and waving their arms frantically from the inside. It was Miss Low." I glance at the teacher. "Really?" The idea of the stiff, formal Miss Low doing anything frantically seems like a stretch. She sniffs, looking a little shamefaced. "We needed help quite desperately," she says, by way of explanation, then busies herself with handing out some buns to the children.

I turn back to Mama. "What happened?"

"There'd been an incident." Mama's face darkens. "Some of the soldiers—they've been shooting into Chinese-owned buildings randomly. Shops, homes, schools. Ethan"— she gestures at the boy on the cot—"Ethan had gone down with Miss Low to get some supplies from the canteen to bring back upstairs for the others. One of the bullets ricocheted off a wall and tore through his shoulder."

I wince at this, looking at the boy's pale, sweaty face, pinched with pain even in his sleep. As I watch, he moves about restlessly, kicking his blanket off. "Is he okay now?" I whisper, not wanting to disturb him. Mama glances at him, biting her lower lip. "No," she says, sighing. "No, he really isn't. I've done as much as I can here, bandaged him up to stop the bleeding, tried to keep him comfortable. But he needs more than that. I need to get him to the hospital."

"Can't we call for help?" I ask. "Don't they have a telephone we can use . . . ?"

"It's not working," Miss Low interjects quickly. "The phone line has been down since this whole mess started. We haven't been able to call anyone. And we daren't go outside because of the . . . well."

I nod, understanding perfectly. Who wants to go outside when you're not sure who will help you and who may kill you?

"All the same, I can't just stand around here watching him deteriorate," Mama says, rubbing her forehead as if it aches. Tendrils of hair have escaped from the bun she usually traps them in, and her face looks worn and gray. She can't have slept in days. My heart swells with worry, and I can feel the Djinn begin to stir. Quickly, I tap my right index finger lightly against my thigh, counting the ornate, patterned tiles set into the floor in threes. I concentrate so hard on this that I barely hear my mother as she continues talking. It's only once I've gotten it right that I emerge from my thoughts into an expectant silence.

"Um, sorry, what were you saying, Mama?"

But she isn't looking at me, she's zoned straight in on my finger. My heart skips a beat. Hurriedly, I jam my hands into my pinafore pockets and rearrange my expression to what I hope is a thoughtful, contemplative look.

"I was saying that they have a van here," Mama says slowly, finally lifting her eyes back up to my face. "The school van, the one they use to pick kids up and send them home. I could go, drive Ethan to the hospital. You'd be safe here with them."

My heart immediately begins to thump in my chest. "I am not letting you out of my sight again," I say. The very idea seems to send a shot of adrenaline through the Djinn, who begins to pace restlessly, sending waves of nausea through me. I feel like I may throw up.

"Now, listen, Melati—"

"No, you listen, Mama." I've never interrupted my mother like this before; it's just not what good Malay girls do. But I think of everything I've done and endured to get to this point, and I'm filled with wild, reckless abandon. I fold my arms and set my jaw, staring her straight in the eyes. "I am not going to be separated from you again. If you want to go to the hospital, then I'm going with you."

Mama sighs in frustration. "Stubborn child."

I turn to Miss Low. "Does the van work, Miss Low? Does it have petrol and everything?"

She nods. "It should," she says. "The driver uses it every day."

"There you go," I tell Mama. "So that's what we'll do. We'll get him to the hospital."

My, my, aren't we feeling brave? The Djinn has been so silent that to hear his voice, low and mocking, is a shock. Right on cue, my head is filled with this journey's possible outcomes, all ending in Mama's death. The nausea returns twofold. I am suddenly, achingly desperate to count something.

I can feel Mama's eyes on me, so I can't tap with my fingers; instead, I tap my tongue against the backs of my teeth, counting each one as I go, first left to right, then right to left. This time I remember to keep my ears tuned to her voice. *Don't let her catch you, Mel. Don't let her see you struggle.*

"We'll have to go as fast as we can so nobody can catch us or stop us," she's saying, tugging her sleeve absentmindedly; it's a habit she has when she's nervous. "I hope I know how to work that thing," she mumbles to herself.

"Why don't we go see it?" I say, heading toward the door. "Then you can take a look, get comfortable with it."

She pauses in the middle of the room, uncomfortable and unsure. "I don't know. . . ."

She glances down again at Ethan as he stirs in the cot, his lips moving feverishly, uttering words we can barely make out.

When she looks up again, her expression is set, determined. "All right." She nods curtly. "Let's go."

It's as we're almost out of the library door that I feel a little tug on my skirt. May stares up at me with huge eyes. "Where are you going, kakak?" she asks, so softly I have to bend close to hear her.

"I'm just going to check on something," I tell her. "I'll be back soon, I promise." Gently, I prize her little hand from the turquoise fabric. "Go wait inside," I say. The door swings slowly shut, and I can feel her eyes boring holes in my back as I walk away.

Five minutes later, we're sitting in the school's dark green van, and my mother is staring at the pedals. "I can do this," she breathes to herself. "I can do this."

"Of course you can, Mama." But she isn't really listening to me; she's too busy checking the gear and peering at the mysterious dials behind the steering wheel. I can understand why she's nervous; Abah taught her to drive ages ago, but he was always the one who took us around in the car. Mama hasn't actually driven on her own in years.

"Just think of Ethan," I say, trying to be helpful. She shoots me a lethal look through narrowed eyes, and I shut up immediately, slinking low in the passenger seat. *She's going to crash it*, the Djinn says knowingly, leaning back in my chest, slowly crushing the air out of my lungs. *She'll kill herself, and you, and that boy while she's at it.* Right on cue, the image comes: The van, crumpled and in flames; our bodies, limp and splayed on the ground. I suck in a breath and exhale slowly, counting rapidly in my head and blinking on every third count, so that Mama won't notice.

"Right," Mama says, interrupting my thoughts, and I quickly sit up, trying to ignore my racing heartbeat. "Right. I think I've got it now. Let's go and get Ethan downstairs quickly."

Soon, we're making our way back to the van, Ethan leaning against Mama and Miss Low while I bring up the rear with an armful of blankets and sheets to try and make the van's hard seats as comfortable as I can. I know he must be in pain, but the boy tries his best not to moan or flinch, and I almost want to cry as I watch him struggle valiantly along, his shirt soaked with sweat.

We settle him as best we can across the back seat, and I tuck a blanket around him so he's nice and snug. "Thank you," he whispers, his voice cracking. "You're welcome," I whisper back, patting his hand and smiling at him.

Mama turns the key and the van's engine rumbles to

life, sending vibrations rippling through the seats. Ethan winces slightly. "Are you all right?" I say, then feel stupid for asking; he's so obviously in pain. But he tries his best to smile sweetly up at me. "I'm okay, kakak," he says, echoing May. *Not for long*, whispers the Djinn.

I give him three quick pats—as much to reassure myself as to comfort him—and slide into the passenger seat, trying to ignore the sick feeling in my stomach. "Ready?" Mama asks me, her eyes fixed on the road ahead, her hands gripping the wheel so tightly I can see her knuckles turn white.

I nod. "Yes."

"All right. Let's go."

I can see the sweat beading on her upper leap, and her lips moving as she recites a prayer under her breath. She switches gears carefully, then slowly begins easing the big van down the road.

BANG BANG BANG.

The noise is sudden and deafening, and I can't help the scream that escapes me, my heart pounding with fear. Mama slams on the brakes, and the wheels shriek in protest. Ethan lets out a deep groan as the van jerks to a stop. "What is going on?" Mama yells. "I don't know, but please, Mama, please don't open the door." I know I'm begging, I know I sound crazy, but my heart is pounding so hard I swear I'm about to have a heart attack, and the Djinn won't leave me alone.

"I have to see what's happening," Mama insists.

"No, Mama, please, let's just go, please, Mama. . . ." I'm sobbing now, hysterical, hanging on to her arm so she can't go anywhere. In my head, a parade of wild imaginings troops past: a shooter appears, blasting Mama's head off with a rifle; looters set fire to the van with all of us still in it; thugs snatch us all out of the van to torture and maim us as they please.

"Calm down, sayang." My mother's voice is low and soothing, yet it's like someone's banged a gong, and suddenly the chaos is gone. Everything is quiet again. "Calm down, sweetheart. It's all right. Just breathe." I follow along obediently, inhaling and exhaling until everything seems right again. "I have to take a look and see what's going on," she says quietly. "I'll be right back."

I can only nod and watch mutely as she swings her door open. I'm too exhausted to do anything else. Instead, I count down the seconds until she returns, leaning my forehead against the cool window beside me, watching my breath create trails of mist that blossom and then disappear again within seconds.

Fifty-two counts later, the door opens, and Mama appears. "Look who I found," she says, smiling wryly. May peeks out from behind her, wearing a shy smile. "Hi, kakak."

"Hi, May," I say, trying my best to hide my frustration.

The last thing we need is another kid to worry about. "What are you doing here? It's much safer for you to be inside, with the other children."

She shakes her head firmly. "No, thank you," she says, like I've just offered her a cup of tea. "I'd rather stay with you." And she hops up into the van and climbs quickly into the back, perching in the seat next to Ethan. "I can help take care of him," she says virtuously, making a great show of tucking the loose corners of the blanket back tightly around the boy. "See? That's better." And she pats him gently on the head for good measure.

I turn to Mama. "Do we really have to take her?"

"We don't have time for arguments," Mama says, climbing in and shutting the door behind her. "We've got to get to the hospital, and quickly. Just be sure to mind us and do what we say, okay?" She directs the last part over her shoulder, and May nods vigorously, looking pleased at not being chased away.

I sigh. "Okay, then. Let's go." The Djinn plays cold notes of fear up and down my spine; in my pocket, my fingers don't stop, the rhythmic tapping muffled by their fabric cocoon.

The first few minutes of the drive are painful. The van grinds and shudders down streets and alleys, but other than a few groans from Ethan, we go on in silence, May and I all too conscious of my mother's gritted teeth, white knuckles, and frayed temper. I keep myself busy counting and tapping and blinking—incantations so that the Djinn will ensure safe passage for all of us.

Eventually, Mama gets the hang of it, and we glide smoothly along the near-empty roads. Behind me, I can hear May humming a little tune, and I feel my own body start to unclench itself. Even the Djinn is silent.

Mama glances over at me and smiles. "Looks like we'll make it," she says, and I smile back because I'm finally starting to believe it.

Until it happens.

There is a strange, uncomfortable clanking from the engine, then another. Mama's face is frozen in a rictus of confusion and panic, and I can feel my own rearranging itself to mirror it. *What's going on? What's happening?* The Djinn immediately rears its ugly head, a smile spreading slowly across his face. *Who said you could stop counting? Who said it was safe? You were careless, and now you'll just have to pay for it.*

"What's happening, Mama?" I cry, but she can't answer; she's intent and focused, gripping the wheel as though her life depends on it—which, of course, it does. As all of our lives do.

If we could keep the van going by sheer willpower, we would have been at the hospital ten minutes ago. As it is, the old green clunker rolls along gamely for a while before slowing, then stopping altogether.

Inside, there is nothing but dead silence. Even Ethan doesn't move a muscle, and for a second I wonder distractedly if he's okay. But only for a second. I'm too busy trying to deal with the Djinn, who has decided to climb onto my back and wrap his arms around my neck; I'm weighed down by dread and fear, and all the air is being choked out of me, painfully and slowly. *You're all going to die here if you don't keep counting,* he whispers in my ear, caressing my hair with long, tender strokes. *Never stop counting again. Never.*

From the seats behind me come the sounds of low, insistent sobbing. Ethan is shaking, tears pouring down his face, sweat soaking through even the blanket that covers him. My mother gets up swiftly to take a look at him, her face grave. "Don't worry, sweethearts," she says gently, addressing us all. "We'll make it there somehow. Not far away now." But I can tell from her expression that she's more worried than she lets on. In my head, the numbers march on in never-ending sequences and ever-mutating patterns, and buried deep in my pockets, my fingers tap so fast you could practically see sparks fly from their tips, if you could see them at all.

"Kakak."

I make no move to answer; the din in my head drowns

out May's timid whisper, and it's taking all my strength to maintain control. I have no energy to spare for chatter, and frankly, I'm irritated at being interrupted when I'm trying so hard to focus.

"Kakak," she says again, more insistently this time. "Kakak. Look." And she tugs at my sleeve, pointing out of the window ahead of us, her eyes wide.

"What? What is it?" I snap.

Then I look.

And freeze.

The van has stalled at the bottom of a low, sloping hill. And coming straight toward us, over the horizon, is a group of Malay men, waving an assortment of homemade weapons, their heads wrapped in red sashes.

There is a roar from behind us, and we whip our heads around. From the back window, we see them: the Chinese men, their own weapons in hand, hurling insults to the Malays. As we watch, one man waves a large broom. "Sweep them out!" he yells, pointing it tauntingly at the group on the hill. "Sweep the useless ones out of here and back to the forest like the animals they are!" The Djinn tightens his grip on my lungs, and I gasp in shock.

It's Frankie. Frankie, waving a broom in one hand and a thick stick sharpened to a three-point spear in the other. Frankie, yelling about getting rid of Malays. Getting rid of me.

I swallow hard and taste bile.

Mama whirls around and our eyes meet. "We're stuck," I say, somehow finding my voice amid the panic rising in my throat. The Djinn begins to pound an insistent beat on my heart, the echoes reverberating through my entire body. "What are we going to do? How are we going to get out of here?" My voice is tinged with hysteria. Mama puts a reassuring hand out to touch my shoulder, but she doesn't say anything. Her face is blank. She has no idea what to do, and I'm almost irrationally angry at her for it. How can she not know what to do? She's an adult! A mother! Mothers are always supposed to know what to do.

"Come on, Mama," I say. "Help me get Ethan down." Between us, we settle Ethan on the floor of the van, a little more hidden from sight, then crouch down with him. Beside me, May presses her little body close to mine, pale and trembling. "It's okay," I whisper to her. "Just stay close to me, and stay quiet." She nods, her eyes wide with fear.

Outside, the two gangs are getting closer—to each other, and to us. The air is thick with tension and shouted slurs, each one uglier and more vicious than the last.

"Stupid Malays!"

"Chinese pigs!"

"Death to the Malays!"

"Go back to China, ungrateful dogs!"

Beside me, May covers her mouth with her hands

to stop the sobs from escaping, tears running down her cheeks. Mama is breathing hard, her hand splayed protectively across Ethan's chest. I shut my eyes tight. *I have to do something,* I think wildly. *I have to save them.*

Too late, the Djinn crows. *You've led them all to their deaths. Nothing good ever comes from caring about you, Melati Ahmad.* The images flash quickly on the backs of my closed eyelids: three dead bodies in the twisted wreckage of a burned-out van.

I double over, feeling like I've been punched in the stomach, doing my best to suck in air.

"What are you doing, Melati?"

I open my eyes. My mother is staring at my hands, where my fingers have been tapping nonstop; they still are, and I can't make them stop. May is staring at me too. "What are you counting, kakak?" she asks me. I hadn't even realized I'd been doing it out loud.

The world seems to shimmer around me, and I grip the seat in front of me tightly to stop from losing my balance. Mama's face slowly crumples. "It's back?" she asks me, and her tone is almost accusing. "The ... visions? The numbers?"

I can't bear to say yes, can't bear to be the one breaking her heart, but the Djinn is so loud I can't even think straight, and I can't break the number chain in my head. All I can do is nod.

I watch my mother grasp for something to cling to, something to hang her hope on, the way a drowning woman flails as the waves engulf her, willing to believe in miracles. Then, slowly, it dawns on her how hopeless an endeavor this is, and right before my eyes, she shrinks and shrivels until there is nothing left in her place but a shell. I see it in her eyes: My mother has lost hope. She has accepted her fate. She is ready to drown.

And suddenly, the Djinn looms before me, dark as smoke and enormous enough to fill the entire world and cruelly beautiful, the edges of his body flickering with blue flame. His raucous laughter echoes through my head. *Look what you did!* He surveys the four of us with satisfaction, breathing in our auras of fear and misery and hopelessness like fine perfumes. *That's that poisoned touch of yours at work again. Your mother is about to die, and she'll die disappointed and ashamed of her only daughter.*

I crumple beneath the weight of his words. Time seems to stop. The barbs come thick and fast, and sharp enough to spill blood. *And it's all your fault, Melati. All of this is your fault. She'd never have been here at all if it weren't for you. She'd never have left the hospital. She'd never have put her life on the line for her useless, good-for-nothing child.*

I can't listen to this. I can't. My stomach is churning, my blouse damp with sweat, and all around me the world is spinning too fast for me to focus. I try to tap, to count, but he just keeps going and I can't seem to block him out. *She's going to die, and it's your fault. She's going to die, and it's your fault. She's going to die, and it's your fault. She's going to die, and it's your fault.*

Your. Fault.

There's nothing more I can do. The mob is right outside our door, and no numbers in the world will save us now.

Let death come. I don't care anymore.

I curl up into myself and squeeze my eyes shut as the relentless waves of anxiety and fear come crashing down on me, pounding me over and over again, dragging me out into a cold and unforgiving sea and leaving me to drown.

Except there is a voice calling me, out there at sea, a voice that sometimes sounds like Saf, and sometimes sounds like Vince, and sometimes sounds like Paul McCartney, and sometimes sounds like . . . God?

Remember how far you've come, the voice whispers. *Remember what you've accomplished. Remember who you are.* Pictures flash through my mind, but this time they aren't images of death. They're images of me: me with Saf, laughing and happy; me with Mama and Abah, our heads bowed in prayer; me helping Auntie Bee hand out food to the neighbors; me with Jay and Vince, ferrying provisions to grateful families; me wrapping Roslan in a sari, our joyous laughter when we realized what we'd pulled off; me approaching armed guards, a determined look on my face, Jee and her baby etched in my mind; me holding May close, protecting her from the mob raging around us.

Me. Just me.

There is a laugh, then, a sound like silver bells tinkling through the air. *You are more than your Djinn,* the voice whispers. *You always have been.*

And then I open them again.

He's gone.

Miraculously, I feel the waves receding, leaving me alone on the shore. The Djinn is silent. In fact—I probe the corners of my mind cautiously, testing all the usual sore spots—he doesn't seem to be there at all.

In his place, a new feeling begins to grow. It's been so long since I've felt other emotions that it takes me a while to recognize what it is, but eventually it dawns on me that it's anger. Bright, blazing anger that is slowly spreading until I am fairly burning with rage at the injustice of our situation. It isn't fair that all we can do is wait for death to claim us. It isn't fair that children like May and Ethan won't have the opportunity to grow up and see the world in all its terrible, wondrous beauty. And it isn't fair that I'll never get to experience a life where the Djinn isn't in charge, where Mama and I can be happy.

And suddenly, before I know what I'm doing, I throw

the door of the van open and slide out, slamming the door behind me, shutting out Mama's cries of protest. I take a deep breath, then turn.

I'm right in the middle of two angry mobs with weapons raised, poised to strike, all looking at me as if I'm crazy.

Luckily, I'm used to that.

"Melati?" Frankie is staring at me, disbelief written all over his face. "What are you doing here?"

"You know this girl?" The question comes from the man standing beside him, muscles rippling ominously beneath his plain white T-shirt as he hefts a large wooden club from one hand to the other and back again.

Frankie sniffs. "You could say that."

"You making friends with Malay scum now, Frankie boy?" The man in white leers at him, and Frankie scowls.

"We aren't friends," he says stonily.

"Then how do you know her?" a voice calls out from the other side, and a young Malay man pushes his way through the crowd, brandishing a parang. "Did you try to hurt her, you filthy dog?" An angry murmur rustles through the crowd. "You keep your nasty hands away from our women!"

"Stop it!" I yell, and miraculously, they do. All eyes are on me.

Deep breaths, Melati.

"I know him because his family helped me when all

the killing and the violence started. They are Chinese and I'm Malay, and they helped me anyway. Because none of that actually matters!"

I look up at the brilliant blue afternoon sky, trying to marshal my thoughts. "Di mana bumi dipijak, di situ langit dijunjung. Have you heard this before? It means where we plant our feet is where we must hold up the sky. We live and die by the rules of the land we live in. But this country belongs to all of us! We make our own sky, and we can hold it up—together."

I look around at the sea of faces, and my heart sinks. Because I can see that I'm not really getting anywhere. I think of Mama, and May and Ethan, and Vince and his parents, and my eyes sting with tears. I turn to Frankie.

"Your ma is the one who taught me that, Frankie," I say, my voice breaking at the memory of Auntie Bee, her warm hugs, her generous smile. "Your mother is one of the kindest, bravest people I've ever met. I never got the chance to say that. You tell her thank you for me, okay?"

Around me, men look at each other questioningly, wondering what to do next. I close my eyes. I don't really care anymore; I've said my piece, and the anger that was driving me has been extinguished. All I want now is some peace and quiet.

"Let's go," a low voice says gruffly in my ear, and I open my eyes with a start, my heart pounding. Frankie is crouched down beside me, grabbing me by the arm and helping me to my feet. "Wh-what?" "Who else is with you?" I gesture to the van, and in a second he's yanked open the door and helping May and my mother, staggering slightly under the weight of Ethan, out. "Come on," he says urgently. "Come on quickly, before they figure out how to react."

The crowd parts slightly for us, still unsure of what to do, and we almost make it out when we hear it. "FRANKIE!" the man in white bellows, an angry vein pulsing in his forehead, his eyes bulging from their sockets. "Frankie, you traitor to your people, get back here!" Frankie ignores them, pushing forward, brandishing his club to ward off any would-be attackers.

The man's yells break the spell, and suddenly the air grows thick with tension. The crowd's low murmurs quickly grow into a roar. "Get your hands off our women, you pig!" one Malay man spits out, trying to grab me by the arm, and I quickly shake him off. Beside me, Mama is panting, trying to walk as quickly as she can with Ethan's arms clasped around her neck. I grip May's hand tightly and try to shield her little body with mine. "Keep going," Frankie says quietly behind us, keeping his parang ready, steadily staring down the hostile crowd.

It's impossible to tell who makes the first move. I hear the clash and scrape of metal and wood, and the crowd explodes. "Run!" I yell, tugging May's arm so hard she almost falls over as we streak down the street, my feet pounding to the same rhythm as my heart. To my right, I see Mama, hanging on to Ethan, matching me step for step with a strength I didn't realize she had. I'm not sure she realized she had it either. But we can't run forever, and I can't think of a plan above the shouts and the *thud*s and the *clank*s and the screams.

Just then, a car barrels down the road and comes to a screeching stop just ahead of us.

But not just any car.

A little gray Standard.

Before I have time to process this, the door is flung open and Vince emerges. "Come on, come on, quickly," he says, taking Ethan from my mother and ushering us all into the car. "What are you doing here?" I ask him as I hoist May into the front seat, then slide in next to her. "Frankie," he says shortly, grunting slightly as he tries to settle Ethan as comfortably as he can, my mother rushing around to the other side to help him. "He was supposed to come with us to Kelantan, but right before we left, he ran off. Ma and Ba got worried—Ma knew he was itching to join the fighting. They made me go out to find him." He scowls, slamming the door shut. "Stupid idiot, making me waste time when I should be getting them somewhere safe. . . . Where is he?"

"He was behind us," I say, twisting around to try and scan the crowd for him. Vince wipes the sweat from his forehead and nods. "Okay," he says. "Lock the doors. Wait for me. I'm going to go look for him. If I'm not back in five minutes, or if it gets too dangerous, get out of here. Don't wait."

"Vince!" It's too late. He's slammed the door and gone before I know it. With trembling fingers, I reach forward and push down the lock, then do the same for all the other doors. The car has stopped, and it's as if we're all just holding our breath and counting down the minutes.

Counting. Counting would feel so good right now. My fingers twitch on my lap, eager to start tapping; I stuff them beneath me and tell my brain to shut up. Now isn't the time to let the Djinn back in.

The minutes seem to stretch on forever, and the noise of the fighting behind us creeps closer and closer. Next to me, May fidgets nervously. "Melati," my mother says, "maybe we should . . ."

"Another minute," I snap back. "Just . . . give him another minute."

The roar of the mob gets louder, closer.

"Melati." Mama's voice is firmer now, more insistent. "We need to go. We need to get out of here, get Ethan to the hospital."

I draw in a deep, ragged breath. I know she's right.

I know we have to leave. But I can't make myself say it. Instead, I just nod, and she gets out and slips into the front seat, gunning the engine. "Hang on, everyone," she says, easing the car into the road.

BANG.

The noise makes all of us jump, and May shrieks, flinging herself into my arms and burrowing her face in my chest. It's Vince, pounding against the window, leaving bloody handprints on every surface he touches. "Let us in!" he yells, and I open the door and leap out.

"Are you hurt?" I say, my eyes frantically raking his entire body for any signs of injury. He shakes his head. "Not me," he says grimly. "Frankie."

I finally tear my eyes away from him to look at Frankie, who is propped against his shoulder, and gasp. Blood flows freely from a gash on his stomach. It's everywhere: smeared all over him, on Vince, dripping onto the pavement beneath them. Frankie's struggling to keep his eyes open; his head dips and lolls as he drifts in and out of consciousness. "Come on," I say, "We have to get him some help."

Together, we play a quick, painstaking game of musical chairs: I move Ethan carefully to the front seat, where he rests his head against Mama's shoulder, May on his other side. Then we settle Frankie into the back seat, his head on Vincent's lap, and I squeeze in next to May, who immediately reaches for my hand and clings to it as if it's some kind of lifeline.

"Let's go, Mama," I say, and she nods and floors it. In the rearview mirror, I watch as Vince strokes his older brother's hair gently. "Don't worry, Kor Kor," he says softly. "Don't worry, big brother. We will be there soon. Don't worry."

As the Standard speeds off, the chaos of Petaling Street behind us and the promise of safety ahead, I swallow the painful lump in my throat and try not to cry.

The rest of it is a blur.

I know we somehow make it to the hospital.

I know the Djinn stirs when we arrive, emboldened by the specters and spectacles of death at every turn. But I also know that I ignore him.

I know there is a great flurry of activity as doctors and nurses whisk Ethan off in one direction and Frankie in the other; Vince takes my hand and holds it tightly for just one moment before he heads quickly after his brother, and the ghost of his touch lingers long after he's gone.

A nurse comes to check May for any injuries, and I have to spend a good ten minutes prizing her hand from mine, convincing her that it's okay to go, that I'll wait for her, that I won't disappear.

And then at last, it's quiet, and it's just me and Mama

under the harsh, flickering fluorescent lights, in a corridor that smells of disease and disinfectant, and maybe even death. Oddly enough, the thought doesn't scare me as much as it used to.

Mama looks at me. "So," she says, drawing in a deep breath, "how was your week?"

And before I know it we've fallen into each other's arms, sobbing and laughing and holding on to each other like we'll never let go.

EPILOGUE

THE TOMBSTONES ARE PURE WHITE, and they gleam with newness in the morning light, the sun's rays playing off the curves and peaks of the headstone and footstone upon which her name is engraved: SAFIYAH, DAUGHTER OF ADNAN AND MARIAM, 3 APRIL, 1953–13 MAY, 1969.

It's my first time visiting her.

I stayed away when she was buried two months ago, unable—unwilling, really—to face Pak Adnan's wrath again. He'll never be able to look at me without thinking of his daughter, without wondering why it is that I lived and Saf died. The least I could do was allow him to grieve in peace.

Instead, I sat in my new room in a house still too unfamiliar to really feel like home, nursing my own sorrow, playing record after record and remembering my friend. Through my haze of tears, I heard my mother speaking to a friend in a low voice. "They were some of the lucky ones," she said. "They have something to bury."

When the hospital was too full of bodies and too caught up in chaos to ensure they were returned to their families, the government had taken drastic measures. They had the corpses carted off and interred into mass graves: one giant hole for everyone, a final resting place crowded with companions. There was no way to protest, and no way to know if someone you loved was one of them. At least Saf's family had something concrete to mourn.

According to the government, the official numbers from that intense, chaotic week, when the city cracked wide open and the streets filled with blood and bodies, are 439 people injured, 196 killed. Auntie Bee and Uncle Chong and Vincent had come to visit the day the report was released, for moral support, Auntie Bee said, though she didn't mention if they were providing the support or needed it themselves.

Frankie didn't come. He never comes with them on these visits, and when we go to their house he makes himself scarce. I'm not sure we'll ever be friends, Frankie and me. But he saved us, and we saved him, and that is a connection that we could never sever, whether we like it or not.

In my room, the Beatles playing softly in the background, Vince squeezed my hand as I heard Mama scoff. "I saw the bodies with my own eyes," she said, tapping the paper in her hand and shaking her head. "No way there were only one hundred ninety-six. No way."

"Must save face mah," Uncle Chong said quietly. He had grown thinner since we'd last seen him, and Auntie Bee limped along with a cane now, a slender, elegant thing of dark wood topped with carved ivory. Mama hadn't wanted me to read it, but I did anyway. Of the dead, the report said, most were Chinese. A handful were Indian. Twenty-five were Malay.

Saf was one of them.

As I stand there, staring at her headstone, I can feel the Djinn stir. *Your fault*, he whispers. *Your fault*. I tap a finger three times against Saf's name, and then I tell him to keep still, and he does. I've come to accept that the Djinn and I are always going to be locked in a battle for control of my brain and my body, that he will never truly go away and leave me in peace. But I also know now that I'm capable of fighting these skirmishes with him each day, and that more days than not, I'm capable of winning them.

I started praying again yesterday.

I kneel down in the dirt, as close to her as I can. "I miss you, Saf. I miss you every day, sometimes so much that it actually hurts." I take a deep breath. "But I'm going to keep fighting, and I'm going to keep living, in your memory. I'll listen to music and laugh out loud, and I'll even watch every Paul Newman movie that comes out, even though Paul McCartney is still the best Paul there is." I can almost hear her laughter, loud and free, in my head. I touch the headstone gently, running a finger once more over the curling Arabic letters that spell out her name. "And we'll meet again, someday, won't we?" I whisper. "You'll wait for me there, and it'll be like we were never apart."

I stand, brushing the dirt from my baju kurung. "I'll come and see you again soon," I promise.

As I walk away, ignoring the lone tear that seems to have leaked from my eye and made its way down my cheek, the sun shines gently, enveloping me in its light, caressing my skin like a blessing.

ACKNOWLEDGMENTS

If your dream is to one day write a book, my wish for you is to have as fierce and loyal an advocate in your corner as my wonder-agent, Victoria Marini, who believes in my words and ideas more than I ever do and is always ready to extend a hand to hold when I need it, or to punch someone in the face in my defense (metaphorically, of course; my agent does not literally go around punching people in the face. At least, not that I know of).

I was blessed the day my editor, Zareen Jaffery, decided to take a chance on an unknown Malaysian writer with an unapologetically Malaysian story. This book is what it is because of her deep understanding of what it needed to be, and the always-on-point feedback it took to get it there. Huge thanks and high fives also go to Alexa, and the rest of the Salaam Reads/Simon & Schuster team, for shepherding this newbie through the book-making process relatively unscathed.

Ribuan terima kasih to Atikah, Arif, and my other beta readers who took the time to help me shape Melati's story into something real and true and book-worthy, and to Deeba Zargapur and my other sensitivity readers, who kept me in check and made sure my depictions of marginalized identities didn't cause unnecessary harm; if you find any inaccuracies within these pages, the fault was mine alone.

Thank you to Morgan, Charlotte, and Ellen, for sharing your stories with me and answering so many of my stupid questions; to Ghaz and Carl, for letting me pick your brains; to Datuk Dr. Andrew Mohanraj, for willingly taking the time to answer my questions on mental health treatment in the 1960s.

I am unbelievably grateful to the brave, brilliant survivors who graciously allowed me to pick through and pull apart memories that were often painful to relive; I'm humbled by your generosity and your spirit. You inspire me.

My thanks to Dipika Mukherjee and Sharon Bakar, who pulled me out of the crowd and made me believe I had stories in me worth telling.

Mak and Abah, thank you for always being ready and willing to help out when I ask. I couldn't have done this without you.

Ibu and Bapak, where do I even begin? Thank you for filling our house with books; for encouraging those first, tentative forays into storytelling; for standing back and letting me pursue these lofty dreams; for believing that I could build a future on words. How can I ever repay you?

I complain constantly about how difficult it is to juggle writing with the wrangling of small humans, but the truth is that I should thank my kids, Malik and Maryam, whose antics and laughter were a much-needed balm to a soul often bruised and battered from wrestling with the intensity of this story. I hope you'll look at this book one day and forgive me for the times I had to leave you with your grandparents or make you wait for ten minutes to play while I furiously jotted down plot fixes or particularly delicious sentences. I hope you know how much I love you.

And finally: To Umar, whose belief in me is unwavering; whose love is constant; whose support comes in a hundred different forms, big and small; who so often and readily utters those magic words: "Go ahead and write, I'll take care of the kids." I love you always and forever.